Mother, Mother, Meat

The Hanging Hill Lane story concludes

Philip Alexander Baker

Development editor: Becker Jones at Jones Novel Editing

Editor: Kathy Towns

Cover artist: Mino

Internal illustrations: Vanessa Baker

Paperback ISBN: 978-1-7392741-4-6

<u>The Hanging Hill Lane Trilogy</u>

The House on Hanging Hill Lane

The Third Hunter

Mother, Mother, Meat

Mother, Mother, Meat

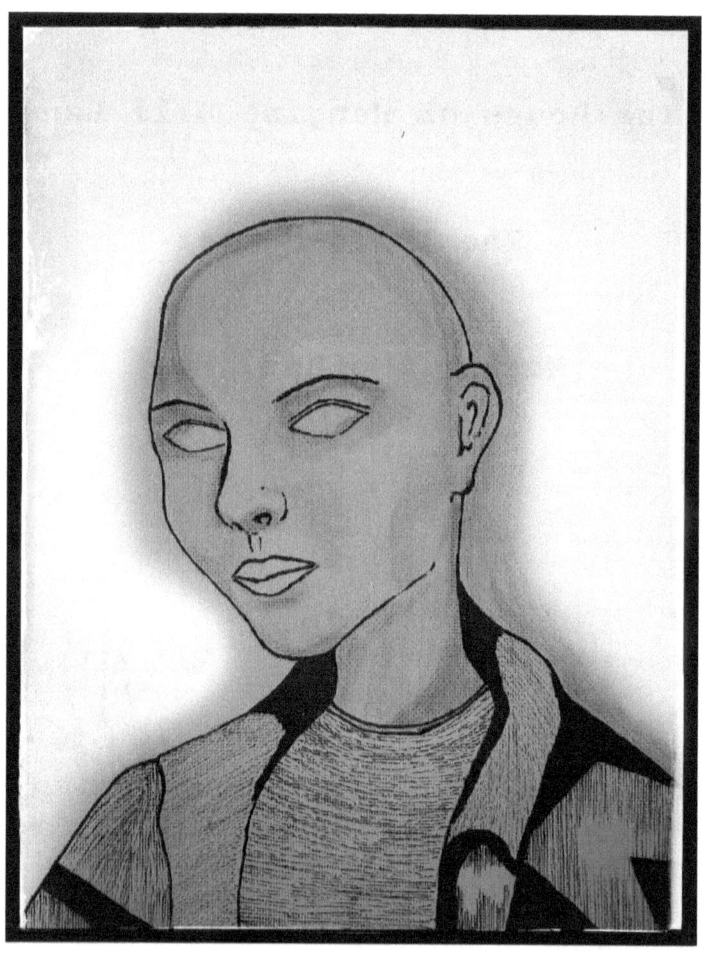

Prologue

'Okay, Doctor Bohn,' she said through her tears.

'My hopes, my dreams, and my deepest, dark fears...'

Part 1

The word on which the whisper turned

Chapter One

THE *CRUNCH-POP-SLAP* OF SARA'S exploding head echoed down the old lane and through the trees as Daphne Locke's world collapsed around her. And yet, now, under the ambulance where she had seen Sara drop, there was nothing.

No dead body. No squashed skull and no blood. No lifeless, headless warm corpse. Daphne had seen Sara's body disappear into nothing in front of her very eyes, gone the same way as the old dead witches before her.

All that remained was clothes on concrete as two panting policemen rushed to the ambulance to slow the vehicle's roll with their broad shoulders and straining legs, shuffling back down the hill as the wheels continued their heavy slow turn. The man next to Daphne grappled with the stone stack that had stood at the bottom of the lane for centuries, sending the smaller stones toppling from the top, and wrestled a large rock up the road as fast as he could, propping it behind a rear wheel of the ambulance, stopping it dead and allowing the other officers to step away and catch their breath.

Daphne watched from the trees, her face frozen, mind racing, and while all she wanted to do was fall to the floor and break into a million pieces, she knew that first she must act. She had a job to do.

"Gotcha."

That's what the voice had said, *gotcha*, it played in her mind again and again, *gotcha*. The demons were there, they were winning, and, *gotcha*, they were right. The word finally stopped its taunting repeats only when the piskie voice rang again through the trees.

'Stupid.'

She fought with her mind and muscles until her face looked something like normal, then hurried over to the policemen at the vehicle just as one crouched down to look underneath. The ghostly white look on his face betrayed how terrified he was of the sickening sight he expected to see. As Daphne crouched alongside him, his mouth dropped and hung.

'She's not there.'

Daphne thought fast. 'Who?'

'The woman. She ran out, went under, I'm sure she did.'

Daphne reached in and snatched out Sara's clothes, the shaking police officer too stunned to stop her. 'I didn't see a woman,' she said. 'I just saw these clothes blowing across from the house. I know whose they are, I'll return them to her.'

A tiny whisper appeared right in her face from thin air, breathy, close. 'Stupid idea.' It was inches away from her. She could smell the warm breath on which the words lingered.

Daphne did her best to block out the words and the freezing breeze that snaked around her neck and into her ear.

The policeman stood aghast. 'I saw her. I'm sure I did. I think.'

'My neighbour? She went back inside.'

The dumbstruck policeman looked to his coworkers, jaw hanging between sentences. 'Did you guys see the mother? I thought she went under. She went under.'

They both looked concerned and crouched down, then one looked back at him. 'No, I just heard the cable crack and ran around to stop it.' He turned to the other police-man. 'Good work with that stone there.'

The shocked policeman shook his head. 'I've heard some pretty creepy stuff happens here, but that was just weird. I could have sworn I saw her. I heard the... the pop.'

'Like he said, brake cable snap,' one said, as he peered under the vehicle at the bare concrete.

Daphne choked. 'Is Alfie, the child...' She knew what the answer would be. Alfie had eaten fish hooks, *hooked* as the demons had promised all along. Now she had one little bit of work to do before she could let the shock hit.

'Huh?' said the policeman, looking around, his jaw fi-nally almost returning to a more normal resting position.

'Oh, the child. I'm not sure I can say anything right now.' He shook his head. 'Sorry, erm, would you mind giving us a few minutes? And look after your neighbour, she'll be needing a friend.'

'A *friend*,' came the chiding whisper from thin air, a deathly smell on the invisible breath. 'Friends don't kill children. And now you are truly alone. Now you have no one.'

Daphne clutched Sara's clothes as she walked back up her own path to the thick wooden door, opened it quickly, and slipped back into number two Hanging Hill Lane, leaving no room between her and the doorframe for anything else to slither in with her.

'No one, alone,' came the voice just as she shut the whisper out.

She pushed the door firmly shut, put her back hard against the wall and slid down with an uncontrolled drop, bouncing painfully on her coccyx, and cried into Sara's clothes. They still smelled of her. A herby smell she hadn't realised she associated only with Sara until now.

Her mind raced, her neurones flying down worn pathways seeking the familiar people she'd always turned to for help, automatically bringing her the most useless and painfully stupid thoughts. Her mother. Gone. Her mind shot to Sara, a most unfair suggestion which came from unstoppable habit. She would always turn to Sara, and Sara would always be there, right up until she had killed her. Everything hurt so much. There was no help now. No hope. No one to turn to at all. She caught herself whispering the truth. 'I'm all alone.'

Alfie. She'd killed Alfie.

The piskie, Charl, had tricked her and she had fallen for it. Now with the clarity of hindsight provided by just a few dark minutes, it all looked so obvious. She had been well and truly stupid, so selfish, and Alfie and Sara had paid the price.

Now, Daphne would pay the price of being all alone.

Panic swept in. Her breathing quickened. The whole world spun as her seated balance started to fail her. Outside, a siren. The wailing, piercing squeal sounded like it was somehow coming from afar, a sound from a distant world that was no longer important and yet was signalling perhaps the most important moment of her life. The beginning of the painful end. As her breathing sped faster, then faster still, her head grew light and her strength and balance abandoned her completely. She dropped onto her side and there was nothing but blackness, the soft fabric of her dead friend's clothes seeming to melt and blend into the wet skin of her cheek. The distant wailing of a siren outside faded away with her consciousness into silence and shadowy black. The last thing to slip from her awareness was the soft scent of Sara's clothes, of Sara, of that unique herby smell that seemed to follow her around, of her friend.

When she woke up, all was dark and quiet.

So very, very quiet.

Chapter Two

DAPHNE SAT UP WITH a jolt, her head full of fog and anger. She still held Sara's clothes tightly in her hand. Groggy confusion made way for clarity the moment the herby smell drifted through her nostrils, and everything that had happened flooded back into her consciousness; *Alfie's dead*, the gut-wrenching emotional pain hitting with it, *Sara's dead*, the strongest of desires rose in her to make things right, to fix it. She was wasting time, and she had very little to waste. She raced into the lounge and dropped the clothes onto the chair.

On the lounge table rested a large brown box. The brand-new mannequin the cardboard contained may have come as a gift of torment from a demon, but it would now serve her. She threw the plastic limbs onto the torso as quickly as she could, smashing the shoulders onto the body with her fist, and as she stared at the headless figure was hit by the agonising memory of what had happened just a few horrible minutes before that played in her head like a high definition movie. *Crunch-pop-slap.* The *crunch* of the skull breaking. The *pop* of the head bursting like a water balloon. The *slap* of the blood and brains hitting the floor. She put the plastic head on fast and dragged the figure upstairs to her mother's bedroom, Sara's clothes draped over her shoulder, and stood it next to the three plastic witches and the mannequin in her mother's clothes.

Five now. Five dead witches.

Quite a collection. Daphne was the last alive.

As she dressed the new plastic in Sara's soft-scented clothes, the shock response finally arrived, it hit her hard and fast. Her breathing quickened again. The dizziness swept back in. The walls appeared to move in closer. Her chest constricted, with the wretched feelings of both being unable to breathe and unable to stop her racing breath. It made no sense. Everything felt confused, and Daphne's hands worked in front of her as though by themselves, dressing the mannequin with the muscle memory formed by months at fashion college.

The moment the mannequin was fully dressed, it looked strangely like Sara. Smelled like her. Felt like her. Daphne ran across the room and flung the window open, desperate for clean air and the slightest breath of clarity. On the dark street below, Alfie's body was being transferred into a second ambulance. The body bag looked so tiny. She wanted to throw up.

Detached voices drifted from below.

'No one's fault, I don't think. Just a terrible accident. That poor mother. Can we get a welfare knock ASAP?'

The voices faded into the back of Daphne's mind as if blown there on a soft, gentle breeze, and her consciousness focused on the gently twirling blue lights below. For a moment, they were hypnotic, and Daphne's mind numbed and blanked and the spinning slowed.

As a growling tow truck rolled down the hill a few seconds later, the words of the paramedic returned to her. *No one's fault.* They marched from the back of her mind to the front and something clicked deep inside. It felt like an epiphany. An epiphany mixed with a new kind of rage, which devoured the feeling of guilt and spat it out with venom. And in that second, just for a moment, she felt like a different person. A stronger one. It wasn't Daphne who had caused this. It wasn't her fault. It was the demons. And the bean-nighe. And Gordon Bright. They did this, not her.

And the piskies.

Charl, the trickster piskie who had given Sara's clothes to Daphne and caused her and Alfie to die. Especially Charl. He did this.

Daphne's hands shook, no longer with fear, pain or panic, but with fury.

Turning around to hide the body bag from her eyes, panic returned, kicking out the anger with a new speed and intensity, her vision softened, and she fell at the cold plastic feet of the row of towering mannequins. She stared upwards, her focus refusing to sharpen. Gugwana, beautifully and colourfully dressed, plastic darkening to a deep brown. Morwenna Rowe, red hair growing. Deanna Tamblyn, eyes that appeared to move.

Her mother. Nothing but plastic.

And now, Sara. Lifeless, unmoving, synthetic Sara.

Daphne lay on the floor at their feet, trying desperately to compose herself. Anger returned.

From the blur above her, a mannequin arm extended towards her. Daphne's focus returned just in time to see the plastic finger of Deanna Tamblyn point into her face as though deep into her soul.

Everything went black.

✳ ✳ ✳ ✳ ✳

A creak from inside the room jolted her eyes open and her mind awake. Just a few inches from her nose, a leather shoe shot into focus. She looked up, ready to defend herself. The mannequins had moved.

All of them.

She was surrounded.

Chapter Three

DAPHNE'S HEART THUMPED AS she lay on the floor with five mannequins towering over her in a circle. The sight of a new mannequin dressed in the clothes of Sara, her best friend, next-door neighbour, and more recently the closest thing she had to a mentor in witchcraft, hit her hard. And yet, an underlying fury made itself known and assured her that she wasn't beaten. A fire still burned. The mannequins stood over her and displayed no body language, no clues to confirm the old witches inside them were still friendly, and though she wanted to trust, it was confusing, their figures intimidating. She would fight back if the mannequins tried to touch her. Except they were friends, surely? Of course they were friends.

As Daphne's body lurched to self-preservation mode, and the moment moved on without any movement from the mannequins, Sara's snuff movie played in her mind again and again, over and over. *Crunch-pop-slap. Crunch-pop-slap.*

Sara had tripped and dropped under the ambulance. But there was nothing to trip over. A voice had whispered in her ear from an invisible source. Yet Daphne had killed the third and final demon, or sent it back to where it came from, or whatever happened to demons when they were slain. It appeared there were still more.

All great things come in threes. The voice of Gordon Bright rattled around in her head. *Including threes.*

Daphne had dispatched three. Three more beaten on the beach by the sirens. Here was the third three. Three more demons. And Daphne was the last witch on Hanging Hill Lane.

Three more.

Gotcha, one had said.

The old house suddenly felt so unsafe, so empty, so devoid of help. She couldn't stay inside forever, allowing in the unbearable guilt and pain that waited for her if she gave them time to strike. But if she were to go outside, the demons would get her. They had whispered. They had killed Sara in front of her eyes. They were out there. Three.

As she lay on the floor gathering her thoughts, the mannequins towering around her, a way out of the pain crept into her mind and whispered.

Just end it all. Kill yourself. The other witches will be safer.

'Fuck off,' she whispered back.

As she pushed herself to her bruised knees, she noticed a white patch of something on her hand. She ran a finger over the substance. A chalky soft dust. She brushed it off and flecks glistened in the moonlight that shone through the window as the dust drifted gently through the air. Daphne followed its slow descent to the floor, and as it softly landed she caught sight of its source. Sprinkled onto the floorboards were five lines of the white powder, connecting each plastic witch to two others, a perfect circle connecting each point.

She had awoken in the middle of a pentacle.

Her head jolted up to the faces of the mannequins. Her mother still looked like shiny, sterile plastic. As did Sara, now just a synthetic statue. But Morwenna Rowe's hair looked longer again, long enough to bounce a little in the breeze, and Deanna Tamblyn's eyes somehow seemed to flicker and shine with life, if only for the briefest of moments. This was a sign. A sign either to say *Hang on, we're coming*, or to say *We're going to make you pay*. The thought was terrifying. A mix of fear and hope. Hope, at last, if just a sliver.

A tiny, tiny, sliver.

She walked around the mannequins, inspecting them closely for signs of change. As she studied the head of Gugwana, she saw something move at the window. A wisp of white drifted past in the air. Daphne ran across and looked down at the road. It was smoke, or steam, or a mix of the two.

A huge vehicle made its way silently down the road, steam and smoke billowing from a chimney, more plumes coming from gaping holes and vents in the sides, so much steam and smoke that it hid the vehicle almost completely, just the corners occasionally poking out, as it floated smoothly past the house without making a sound. Ash blew by the window as the vehicle disappeared into the woods. Impossible. There was no way a vehicle that big could get through those trees, through the remains of the stone stack. Yet she watched it do just that.

'What the hell was that?' whispered Daphne.

You know, though, don't you? came an unexpected thought.

Oh no, came a young voice from deep within.

Chapter Four

NOTHING WOULD GET IN through the front door; the old, thick wood barely budged as Daphne thudded her palms into it, feeling its strength. The old engraved iron bar slotted neatly into the heavy mounts.

The back door and old windows were as thick and safe as ever, and she had double- and triple-checked every one. She wasn't going to make a rookie error now, however tired she was. Every possible opening to the house was checked, every chance of entry blocked. But no sooner had a feeling of safety dared to hint at itself, she caught a glimpse of movement from the corner of her eye; something was in the lounge with her. She spun around, dreading what she might see lurking in the dim corner, and breathed relief when she saw what had moved: just the mirror, her reflection slinking by like a shadow of herself.

That old mirror held such memories. Her mother had played peekaboo in it while under the influence of the witch's love salts, and that thought was the closest she had come to smiling for a while. She'd checked and squeezed her spots and acne in it as a young teen, jumped up with joy to get a glimpse of her laughing face as a child. And now there she was, staring at her own exhausted and ghost-white expression staring back at her. It looked like the face of someone who had killed her friend and her child. The face of someone who needed to be punished. The face balled up and turned angry. Daphne made a tight fist and threw a hard punch. The punishment had begun, the punishment of the stupid girl in the mirror.

She barely felt the pain in her knuckles as she punched and punched, shards of glass showering onto the carpet around her feet. She punched and punched again until there was barely a sliver of glass left, just the blood-covered wooden backing, thick glass splinters sticking out of her bleeding knuckles, sharp shards lying on the floor. When she'd finished her assault on the mirror and the girl who had been inside it, she caught herself picking up the fallen frame, instinctively looking through it as though the glass remained intact within. But there was no reflection, no face. Just a bloody frame and splintered backing, which she smashed against her face, taking the pain she deserved. She sank to her knees amongst the glass. The same glass that had given her some of her favourite and most innocent memories, which was now shattered and scattered on the carpet around her, cutting into her bloody knees and poking out of her wet red hands. She rolled down onto the floor, a broken person with nowhere to run and no one left to help her. At least her reflection wasn't there to watch now, no stupid bitch in the mirror. At least she'd started her punishment. Someone had to suffer for what had happened to Alfie.

Daphne's eyes stung but they remained wide and staring, her energy was depleted and her head felt light yet too heavy to move. She took in the room from her position on the floor, her perception skewed by the angle at which her head lay and the tears in her eyes. The walls gave the impression they were closing in on her again. What used to be so familiar now felt odd and angry, what felt so safe now felt full of danger. Anguish built up inside until the pressure became unbearable, and the only release was a desperate, throat-shredding, wailing primal scream from the depths of her lungs and soul, so long and rough and loud it left her ears ringing and the chandelier swinging, moving and bending the shadowy shapes around her on the wall, making a spider running across the room through the sweeping shadows appear as a giant. As the echo of the scream faded, so too, just a little, did her pain.

She stared vacantly at the spider, who had paused his journey across the wall and seemed to stare back. A thought crawled forward from the recesses of Daphne's mind with a message: *there's a better way*. She had learned some skills to deal with times like this. Not from her mother, or the textbooks or any other witch, but by a human named Doctor Bohn. Immediately, everything felt very different.

After the killings two years before, the authorities had offered counselling to Daphne, and she had been to see Doctor Bohn several times. He would teach her coping strategies for the worst of times. One of them was very simple. And so she got to her bleeding feet and strained her mind just to look, to see, to almost feel. To make things better.

'Curtains,' she said, looking at the old moth-eaten material draped in front of the locked windows. The curtains moved slowly, unnaturally. Her voice wavered, a mere whisper, and she looked for another object. 'Sofa.' The technique was simple: get her attention on something in her immediate reality – and therefore out of her mind and horrible thoughts. 'Carpet.' Her voice picked up a little volume. 'Smashed mirror.' She felt the hope of momentum and raced to spot something else. 'Textbooks. Door.' She looked at her hands. 'Blood.' This wasn't working. 'Dinner table. Dinner table full of crap.' Definitely not working. Rage boiled up. 'Full of pointless fucking crap!' She flew towards the dinner table with a yell and swept everything onto the floor. Cups and books came crashing down onto the carpet, the thuds and smashes they made drowned out by Daphne's scream that went on and on until there wasn't a hiss of air left in her lungs. And then the table went over, thrown to the floor with another shout so loud it brought more pain to her already burning throat.

And then she felt it.

The knobble.

Poking up below her was something hard and rounded, raised from the floorboards under the carpet, pushing into the arch of her bare foot. *The knobble.* The feeling took her back fifteen years or more in a second, stopping her turmoil in an instant. The knobble felt like an old friend, one she hadn't even thought of for as long as she could remember. As she rolled her bare foot around on the bump in the carpet, everything came flooding back.

When she had been small enough to stand under the dinner table, she used to hide underneath, feeling safe and having fun, and she'd often feel the knobble under her foot. It was just a part of standing under the table, little Daphne's hiding place, a place she thought of as her own. Part of her childhood.

When little Daphne was standing under the table when she was in trouble or worried she might get caught, she would push her foot down on the knobble, and the feeling of it would make things a little less scary. Feeling the knobble under her foot was somehow comforting. Sometimes Sara's mother would be round chatting to her mum, and then she always felt scared because she was such a big, intimidating, outright scary woman. Where other kids had a comfort blanket, little Daphne had her knobble. She hadn't even thought about it since the day she grew too tall to stand under the table. And now here it was, saving Daphne at twenty.

Wow, the knobble still felt exactly the same. Except now, it was transformed with the added magic of a beautiful but bittersweet nostalgia for a lost childhood. A lost mother. A crumbling home. And yet the knobble did bring her hope.

That feeling under her foot felt like a reason to live. It felt like childhood.

With the feeling of the hard round bump in the arch of her foot, she found herself calming, breathing easier, relaxing. There was no way that small loving child would have let her get into a state like this. It was like the child was coming back to rescue the young adult in her moment of need.

The broken mirror. That child had loved that mirror.

She stumbled into the bathroom, the feeling of the knobble still fresh in her foot. She turned on the tap and ran her hands under the water. A stream of bloody red swirled into the plughole. As the water flowed, she slid out the glass shards from her fingers, knuckle by knuckle, splinter by splinter. Each one stung, and after each jolt of pain, she took a sharp breath to prepare for the next. A large glass piece had pushed itself up under her fingernail, and as she slid it out, she sucked in a huge gasp with the quick squirt of blood. It wasn't until all the glass was gone and the water running down the plughole was almost clear again that she looked up, straight into her own eyes in the bathroom mirror. But this time, she wasn't angry at the person she saw. This time she hated what had done this to her, what had made her the tired, pained wreck looking back at her. That little girl who loved the knobble deserved better. And then she felt something rush back to her, as she stared back at herself.

She felt it in her gut.

Her breathing deepened and slowed. Her eyes focused. And, never breaking eye contact with the witch in the mirror, not distracted by her prickling skin nor the blood that oozed from her knees, never blinking as her vision tunnelled in on the face in the reflection, barely recognisable as it seemed to morph into a new person, a fighter, a warrior, that warrior spoke five words. And in that moment, oh how she meant those words, how she knew them to be true.

'I'm gonna hurt those fuckers.'

A shrill cackle pierced the walls. She'd heard that cackle before.

Piskies. They were back.

This time there was no fear.

She pulled an alcohol wipe from the cupboard and cleaned the blood from her knees. The sting did not bother her, nor did the sight of her blood. The next blood she saw would belong to the piskies. She had nothing left to lose. She would find a way.

The laughter continued through the cold air, but in Daphne's head, the cackle fell silent, and the world was tinged with red.

Chapter Five

THE VIEW FROM THE window revealed nothing. There was quiet inside and outside the house. The piskies weren't getting too close, not crawling out of the woods. She would not charge out at them in a rage. She would not fall into a trap. 'Take a breath and be clever,' her mother used to say.

Daphne sought control, information, anything at all to move forward. The human television news was often a useful source to find out what was going on, a quick place to start. She used to think it was a stress response inherited from her mother – putting the news on to distract herself in times of trouble – but now it made sense. When Mum was stressed it was because something bad was going on, and when that kind of *something* was going on, someone not too far away would invariably end up horribly dead. The humans would dutifully report it. It was an obvious and weirdly useful source of intel. The TV news was her mother's way of taking a breath and being clever.

When the TV fired up, Daphne's prayers were answered immediately. The news was reporting that the missing child Penelope Pengilly had returned alive and well, and in a strange twist of events, had been found by another woman police were searching for, Olivia Merrigan.

Olivia.

Olivia the truffle pig. Olivia the demon hunter. Olivia, Daphne's friend. Hope hit her hard and fast and she grabbed at her pockets, frustrated with the reminder that her phone wasn't there, smashed up by the demon inside the girl whose picture was now on the television. She grabbed her laptop and tried the call function on the messenger app.

The tone seemed to ring for an eternity before it cut.

She tried again. Still nothing. And again.

She gave up calling, and went to her last hope for some kind of help. She walked into her mother's bedroom, turned the mannequin dressed in her mother's clothing to face her, looked at its plain, plastic face, and felt the disappointment sink in. 'I beat some demons, Mum. I could just use some help to beat a couple more.' The silent reply was deafening. The moment seemed to stretch, so quiet and empty.

Everything felt still, lonely. And yet she felt the flicker of fire in her burn.

Take a breath and be clever.

Her quiet breath was amplified by the silence of the old house.

One breath. Two breaths. Three breaths. Four. Simple, simple breathing.

Until there came a tapping on the downstairs window.

Something creaking.

Something sneaking.

A tap-tap-tapping on the downstairs window.

Chapter Six

Tap-tap-tapping on the downstairs window.

A screeching scratch right through the door.

It stopped and the world went quiet.

Then the finger tapped some more.

CRACK! A whack on the window a few feet from Daphne's face forced her to wince and flinch and squeeze her eyes hard. When they opened again, Gugwana's mannequin had turned its head a full quarter turn, now facing the window, its still plastic body otherwise as stiff and lifeless as ever. And then the tapping downstairs started again and something else cracked hard against the glass.

The doorbell chimed, then chimed again. The tapping stopped, then the laughs began. Cackling laughter from outside in the distance, growing closer, voice by voice, until one laugh was indistinguishable from the others, a growing chittering crowd of cackling and snickering voices right outside. They stopped suddenly and together.

All fell quiet and Daphne's world paused; the finger of silence tapped her on the shoulder and reminded her she was alone.

A thin voice from outside seemed to waft to her window on the breezy air.

'Daphneeeee,' it called. She knew that voice. It had spoken to her before. It had called out from the woods the moment after the ambulance had crushed Sara. It had called her stupid.

All fell still and her heart pounded through the silence that followed as she breathed quietly through rounded lips.

She stepped towards the window, ignoring the ghostly reflection that stepped towards her, knowing how that glass would protect her as it had protected the house for nearly two hundred years. Whatever was out there, she would be safe from it, in the immediate moments at least.

She slowly pushed her head near the glass. *Crack!* A stone ricocheted off the glass leaving a loud bang ringing through Daphne's mind as she jerked her head back.

She leaned forward and peered out of the window into the dark night. A light mist of rain fell, creating a golden glow under the dim old streetlamp. The police and ambulances were gone. In their place, were the piskies.

Lots, and lots, and lots of piskies.

Shit, that's a fuck load, whispered the voice of her mother from deep inside her mind.

Creatures huddled from the rain under a shredded umbrella. Some danced and laughed on the road. Most just stared back up at her, stupid grins on their horrible little faces. A fat one waddled like a toad. As she scanned the crowd of three-foot-tall creatures dressed mostly in green, one stood out immediately. Wearing dark red with a leafy belt and pointy hat, it stood in the middle of the street, staring at her, a circle of space around it where the other piskies apparently dared not stand. This one carried itself like a leader. It opened its mouth and called.

'Daaphneeeee.'

That was the voice. That was the piskie. And then walking from the crowd into the vacant circle around the piskie in red, came another. This one was instantly familiar, though it moved differently from before. It wasn't timid like the last time they had met. It walked confidently, cartoonish in its proudness. Its round eyes bulged as they made contact with Daphne's. The piskie smiled, its pointed teeth glinting in the streetlamp light, and Daphne's fists balled tightly.

Charl.

Charl had done this. Charl had tricked her into causing the deaths of Sara and Alfie. Charl had feigned being the good guy, all part of a bigger plan. He was the same as the rest of the piskies who had chased and terrorised her. Worse. Charl was worse.

Charl was going to have to pay.

If only there wasn't an army of piskies outside to stop her from getting to him.

'Shit,' she mumbled to herself as she stared out of the window as a one-armed piskie climbed halfway up the old lamppost and slid back down with a grin, letting out a little laugh, just before another rock bounced off her window with another deafening *CRACK!* Daphne looked over her shoulder at the figures behind her. 'Gonna need you soon please, ladies.'

Gugwana's mannequin's head turned towards her, and smiled, and Daphne's mouth dropped. Her head shot to the right, checking a different mannequin.

Her mother's plastic head stared straight forward, still, lifeless.

Synthetic Sara reflected the light, ever so softly.

Outside her house was all the evil, all the creatures behind the deaths of the people who once wore these clothes. Hatred spilled into her gut. A hard, overpowering hatred. It was a new feeling, and she knew exactly where it was directed. At that little shit outside. Charl. Fucking Charl. She hated him.

Really hated him.

Perhaps it was the tiredness, or the fact that she had no hope and no reason to be nice to anyone anymore, but she felt a new desire fill her. The desire to see Charl suffer. The *need* to see Charl not just die, but suffer. Suffer horribly as he died. She pushed her face back up against the glass, and the piskies fell quiet and still as they stared back. Daphne made eye contact with Charl, who smiled and waved back like an old friend. The little shit.

Another stone cracked the window an inch in front of her nose. Daphne didn't flinch, didn't even blink as she glowered back at Charl, picturing all the ways she'd like to hurt him. Words began to gestate on her tongue. Words that had terrified her once before. Now, on her own lips, they felt perfect. She smiled menacingly down at Charl, and mouthed the words gently, her breath forming a round smudge of condensation on the window in front of her face.

'You. Will. Burn.'

With a stiff finger, she drew a line in the condensation. Then another. Then another until the pentacle was complete.

She was sure she saw Charl's smirk fall from his face, if only for a second. And then it returned, and he pulled something small from his pockets and held it, no, them, up in the soft light. Mittens. Alfie's little red knitted mittens. A reminder of what she'd done. He smiled and his teeth poked above his lower lip. A second later, holding the red mittens aloft, he danced. He moved gleefully, holding dead Alfie's mittens up high, never breaking his gaze from Daphne, never dropping his grin. Charl. He had done this. He had tricked her by pretending to be her friend. He had killed Alfie and Sara. And now he was mocking her. He was mocking *them*, the dead.

Charl's dancing legs looked so small. So thin. So snappable. As did his stupid little neck.

A shriek pierced the air from the woodland. Daphne looked to the wood's edge, and there she was. The bean-nighe stared back up at her with her disgusting face. Daphne could see the hag's vast shoulders bounce up and down. She was laughing. She'd done this too, and now she was there, mocking her with the piskies.

It was a horrible feeling, a mix of rage and utter helplessness and hopelessness. The rage meant nothing when logic told her she was massively outnumbered, even if her heart and anger disagreed. The rage powered Daphne's scream through the window, her voice painful and hoarse as the sound bounced back loudly from the glass. As her scream faded, her ears rang. The piskies all broke into chiding laughter.

The thought of opening the front door and charging out armed with a sharp kitchen blade and taking out as many little shits as she could didn't seem like a bad idea. Suicide by piskie. At this stage, why the hell not? Her mother had owned a massive butchering machete that would do the job nicely.

The deep anger inside her was demanding to be satisfied. To see Charl a quivering wreck, begging for forgiveness, desperate for his life. To send back those damned demons that had killed Sara and Alfie. And her mother. They'd killed her mother. And then there was the bean-nighe. She needed a good hard kick in her disgusting gut, a fast fist in her disgusting face before her head was removed.

Revenge would be so, so sweet.

The only thing stopping her was the brutal reality of the situation, of being a five-foot-two young woman with no powers to speak of, of being completely alone.

She moved back away from the window and against the wall and put her head in her palms, and caught her head shaking, her breathing quickening, too fast, losing control, not sure if the feeling was panic or anger.

She quickly thought back to the techniques Doctor Bohn had taught her to avoid attacks like this. She closed her eyes and flooded her mind with an image. What came was beautiful. It was her with Paulie, living in peace by the beach. Coconuts hanging on trees over the sand. Picture-perfect. The weirdest thought hit her. *Why not?* If she simply called a taxi, the creatures would flee from the human eyes as they always did, and she could just go. Pack her bags, call Paulie, apologise and invite him on holiday, make the bookings, call a cab, and *just go and never come back*. How good that felt. Just that one little thought had reversed her oncoming panic attack. Sure, there was a very good chance she would be followed and slaughtered at the first opportunity, but also, maybe she wouldn't. Maybe it could work out, all those miles from home, away from the demons and the piskies. It was comforting and tempting.

But, as she opened her eyes and another cackle pierced the air, she had another, conflicting thought: going out in a machete-driven blaze of piskie blood was just as tempting as the peace of a distant seashore.

A moment of clarity, a realisation that hit her like a tree branch to the head: this was a genuine decision to make. She could, and would have to, literally do one of these two things. Just two options, two possibilities. It seemed that not everything came in threes after all.

Revenge.

A peaceful life, if she wasn't murdered as she ran.

Revenge.

Coconuts on the beach, but probable death. A death on her terms, accepted, in pursuit of a better life. Or some revenge and the certain death that came with it. Either way, death seemed even more probable as a hammering on the door and downstairs windows built into a chaotic drumroll from Hell.

Daphne found it hard to make a decision where both outcomes were likely her death. And once again, she remembered some advice from her mother, who, even in death, always seemed to be around when she needed her the most.

'Spin a coin,' she'd once said. 'And in the moments before the spin dies, you will know at heart which way you want the coin, and your decision, to fall.'

Great. Her method of death was going to come down to the toss of a coin, or the decision she made in the seconds before it landed. Still, that was better than the anguish of sitting slumped against a wall for hours or days working out the best way to die as hundreds of creatures mocked her from outside.

CRACK! Another rock on glass.

She opened her mother's drawer and grabbed a coin that she had always known was special. Her mother had said it was pure gold, and never for spending. It held other values, she had said. Now, finally, Daphne knew what the large, old gold coin was for. She took it into the privacy of her bedroom away from the eyes of the mannequins, away from the piskies cackling on the road outside. She slid the books off her desk and onto the floor, placed the edge of the coin on the surface, and gripped the cold metal hard between thumb and forefinger, her finger muscles taught and ready to spin it on the desk.

Time to find out whether she was to be almost certainly murdered in pursuit of a peaceful life, or succumb while bloodily carving her way through the sea of piskies. The idea of revenge still felt good. Charl. And that leader in red. The washerwoman bitch. She'd carve them all up with a smile if that's what the coin commanded. If only she'd had a flamethrower, she'd burn the lot of them.

She took in a breath, and everything stood still.

'Heads, I pack up and go. Tails, it's knife time.'

She leaned back.

She spun the coin hard.

It flew quickly off her desk and onto a pile of dirty clothes and stopped, edge straight up.

She retrieved the coin, placed it edge-up on the desk again, and spun.

This time, it stayed true and steady as it spun, a soft grinding sound emanating from the whirling coin as it made circular motions around the wooden surface.

'Heads I just go,' she whispered, 'painting on the beach until I'm old.' She smiled at the thought and the world felt a little better. 'Tails, kill them all.' She felt something stir in her stomach as the words left her lips. Maybe that would be her choice as the coin started to slow.

She closed her eyes. And there, inside the darkness, she immediately saw her decision as clear as day. Images flashed bright and clear. The beach looked so peaceful. She saw herself sitting on a stool on the sand with her easel, painting, miles away from the pain of Hanging Hill Lane. When she saw the image of Paulie walking up to her on the sand, embracing her from behind as she painted, she blubbed an unexpected tear, taking her by surprise. She felt it there and then. Running was no good. She couldn't take Paulie – the risk of them both being chased down and slaughtered was far too great – so what was the point? Life was about living on her terms, and that had been taken from her. No. She would step outside and slaughter piskies until she fell. She had nothing else to lose or give.

She opened her eyes, ready to catch the coin on its dying spin.

Except the coin wasn't slowing. Far from it. It spun there on the desk, seeming to almost speed up with every rotation. It just spun.

And spun.

And spun.

And spun.

And Daphne, as though commanded by the hypnotic whirring of the swirling coin, plummeted into sleep.

* * * * *

Daphne sits in a grey, dank room amongst the dead bodies on the chairs. In front of her, the back of her dead mother's head as she sits, still and lifeless.

As she had as a child, Daphne brushes her mother's hair, and as she combs it back from the dead forehead, her dead head flops back with it, her dead eyes open and, still dead, very dead, the eyes look at Daphne. She closes the eyes with the palm of her hand and pushes the head forward and continues to brush her hair.

The funeral is coming, coming soon, finally. She has to make her look nice as only she knows how to do. The time has come. She has been waiting for this for so long. She brushes her hair some more, and then starts to braid, for this is a special occasion, her last goodbye.

When she accidentally touches her mother's head, it feels cold. But inside her stomach, Daphne feels warm. Finally, an end. Finally, the chance to do one last thing for the mother she had loved so much. The braids are looking pretty, and Daphne smiles.

The morgue door opens.

Into the room waddles the bean-nighe, and dread pushes out any good feeling from the dream; dream turns to nightmare; the bean-nighe approaches Daphne and her dead mother, and speaks in that wretched voice.

'A question for a question.'

The bean-nighe is upon her, inches away.

Daphne punches her, smacks the ugly face, but the blow does nothing, nothing at all, and the bean-nighe pushes Daphne helplessly to the floor. Daphne tries to stand, tries to strike back, but her legs just don't move, and the bean-nighe laughs her disgusting laugh and grabs at her mother's hair, pulling it, yanking it, her whole head locked in her other arm.

'Let her go!' cries Daphne.

The washerwoman looks up, smiles back at Daphne's face, and dribbles as she says in a child's voice, 'No, you.'

Daphne shouts back, 'No, you!' and her voice is that of a child's.

Daphne's mother's dead head spins around in the washerwoman's grip and spine bones crack and pop, her eyes open and she says to Daphne, 'No, you,' and the bean-nighe grins and rips off the hair and scalp of Daphne's dead mother, whose eyes, nose and mouth all close and seal shut. The fucking bitch! The anger. The helplessness. The end.

✳ ✳ ✳ ✳ ✳

When she awoke, dazed, confused and angry, the sun was shining brightly through the curtains and the sound of spinning metal on wood still murmured from the top of her desk.

She squinted as her thoughts cleared and slugged through the sleepy grogginess.

She looked at her clock. Hours had passed.

The coin was still spinning with no sign at all of slowing down.

Daphne stared at it and caught some words leaving her mouth as if spoken by someone else, and then recognised the words as a common phrase her mother had used. It had almost sounded like her mother's own voice.

'Buggered if I know,' she said, and walked down the stairs, into the kitchen, opened a drawer, and stroked the handle of the biggest, sharpest, heaviest knife in the house.

Chapter Seven

Daphne peered around the lounge curtain. Outside was strikingly normal, aside from her wheelie bin on its side on the wet road, a small, cylindrical turd lying thereon, gently rolling back and forth in the wind.

She scoured the familiar view for signs of anything unusual or threatening. It all looked so quiet. Pushing her head against the glass, she looked down the hill to the edge of the woodland. She saw it just before it disappeared back into the undergrowth. A piskie. They were still there, watching, just concealing themselves now without the cover of darkness. Perhaps she could pick them off one by one. The idea felt satisfying.

Before she opened the door, she felt the urge to one last time switch the television on. Perhaps to say goodbye to

37

the world outside Hanging Hill Lane, the last time she would see it.

You're dallying, came the voice of her mother in her head. 'Take a breath and be clever, Mum,' Daphne whispered back.

Daphne knew the programme would be filled with the horrors of a dead child who had eaten fish hooks, and then likely the news about his missing mother, if anyone had tried to find her. The pain would be almost unbearable. But it felt like she had no choice, like she had to know.

Daphne sat down in front of the TV, dread filling her stomach.

Alfie. Alfie was the news. But the story was not about the tragic death of a local child who had eaten fish hooks. It was so much worse.

Reporter Angela Shipman spoke of the death of a local mortuary worker who had died in suspicious circumstances, police not yet releasing any details. Apart from one: the body of a child he had been with had gone.

Police believed that someone had broken into the morgue and killed the man and stolen the child's body. Daphne knew exactly whose body that would have been. And she knew it wasn't a human that stole it.

Poor Alfie. The demons couldn't have got any more disgusting, more grotesque if they had tried, and Daphne felt a new kind of pain in her gut. It felt hot.

But why would the demons want Alfie's body?

The picture that followed in her mind made her bend over and throw up a wave of vomit, visions of the demons ripping apart Alfie's body in front of her. It was coming.

She was convinced of it, and her nervous system responded with wretches and coughs and throwing up until there was nothing left to throw up, leaving her a breathless wreck.

As the coughs and wretches subsided, the faint whirr from the spinning coin upstairs gently cut through the silence.

But she needed more, and the human news often told only part of the story.

Daphne panted and spat as she fired up her laptop and headed for social media. Often, what wasn't said on the news was said by people in the know, a few strands of genuine knowledge amongst hundreds of idiots speculating and throwing out conspiracy theories. But if there was anything more to know, and anyone had known it, someone somewhere would have posted online about it. She loaded up the site and searched for the terms *missing child*, *morgue*, and *dead*. Instantly hundreds of search results appeared from the last few minutes.

What she saw disgusted her.

Jokes. Joke after joke about the missing body of the baby, and the man who had died doing his job. Humans really were revolting. Then as she scrolled, two words jumped out at her.

Fish hook.

She braced herself and read the whole post. Someone here knew something.

Don't talk shite, it's true. My mate works at the morgue where it happened. Poor guy was found dead with a fish hook in each eye. So shut your mouth, cocksucker.

A fish hook in each eye. She clicked to see the post it was replying to. She didn't recognise the name. It simply said, WTF IS GOING ON AT THE MORGUE IN ST AUSTELL? APPARENTLY, SOMEONE HAS NICKED A KID'S CORPSE AND KILLED THE GUY LOOKING AFTER IT. I CALL BULLSHIT, LOLZ.

The coin sounded like it was getting louder.

A word whistled through her mind in a whisper-turned-guttural voice of a demon, a recording-like memory of the creature that had climbed on her two years before. *Stupid*, it had said. *You stupid little girl, alone.*

Stupid.

Even in her head, the memory sounded so real.

Stupid. It had been the word on which the whisper turned. Her life had turned direction with it.

WTF? Those three letters from the social media post came back to her. *WTF.* A tip from Sara about gathering info when things turn weird – get onto social media and search for recent posts with the term *WTF.* Humans always wrote that when things got weird. As always, hundreds came up, but it was always worth scrolling down for a while. When the demons were around, someone was always on social media typing *WTF* about it.

MY MRS WAS HAVING IT AWAY WITH THE PIZZA DELIVERY GUY. LIKE I LIVE IN ACTUAL PORNO. WTF! said one.

She scrolled faster.

And then, there it was, the thing that caught her eye. A photograph.

It was black and white, a screengrab from a CCTV camera, a little unclear. It was a child, a young boy, the shot taken from behind. The child was completely naked, gripping a huge stick, smashing it into a shop window, the child's naked bum blocked out by a superimposed giant yellow laughing emoji.

Daphne zoomed in closer on the back of the head of the boy. The pixelation got worse the more she zoomed in, but she was as sure as she could be. That distinctive tuft of blonde hair. Alfie's. Her eyes focused in on the caption. MY WORK'S CCTV GOT THIS TONIGHT. NAKED KID SMASHING OUT OUR FRONT WINDOW. WTF!

Alfie was *alive*. Impossible.

Daphne clicked the poster's profile and scrolled through his posts, scouring them for info on where he worked, information that would tell her where Alfie was seen. Nothing. She tried a search engine, copying and pasting in the name. And there it was. Shop assistant at Kenny's Shop of Horrors.

It was a shop in St Austell, the town where Alfie had gone missing from the morgue. Alfie, at two years old and reportedly dead, was smashing the window in a kid's costume shop.

Daphne's heart cracked into two. Half filled with relief. Alfie was possibly alive. Somehow.

The other half flooded with despair. If he was alive, and smashing shop windows when he was barely old enough to walk, he had strength far beyond that of a human toddler.

There was only one explanation. A demon had taken Alfie.

A quick web search for Kenny's Shop of Horrors: masks, fun costumes suitable for Halloween or theatre productions. If someone wanted to dress up as anything at all, Kenny's Shop of Horrors had it. The demons seemed to want to get some clothes on Alfie's little body.

It didn't matter that she didn't know where Alfie and the demon were. It knew where she was. All she'd have to do was wait. And, as she waited, she simply needed not to let herself break under the sea of pressure that the demons and their minions outside were going to joyfully exert. If Alfie was alive, then everything had just changed. This was now a rescue mission.

She knew exactly what she needed to do to pull that demon from Alfie when it arrived. She needed to get hold of Olivia and draw it out, just like the day before with the demon in Penelope Pengilly.

She messaged Olivia through her laptop, and watched the single *sent* tick sit by her message. Olivia's phone wasn't even on. 'Damn you, Liv,' she whispered to her screen.

There wasn't another plan that felt like it would work. But if she was to sit idly and wait, tired, hurting and worrying, stewing in the madness, she would be playing into the demon's hands, or claws, or tentacles, or whatever this one had. She needed something to cling onto while the demon found her. Some hope that she could win without Olivia if she didn't make it in time.

Demons. Three. And an army of piskies.

No witches to help.

No Sara.

No Olivia, at least for now.

There was just one person in the world who might know anything, even if she did hate him for what he had done. So she ordered a taxi to ensure there wouldn't be any meddling piskies outside, and stopped dallying.

She brought up the taxi firm's website and keyed in her destination: Gwydhenn Centre Psychiatric Hospital.

It was time to pay a visit to a man she truly hated. The thought of him, his peeling cheeks and arrogant smile, made her skin crawl. The only human she had grown to truly despise. But with a demon on the way in Alfie's skin, she had to go, she had to see the only human she would quite like to see dead. The only one who may be able to help.

The once-Detective Inspector of the local police force.

Gordon Bright.

Chapter Eight

DAPHNE MOVED AWAY FROM the house towards the waiting taxi, one eye always on the woods for the piskies, the rest of her senses on high alert for any sign of any kind of invisible presence. She slid into the back of the taxi, closed the door, and watched the woodland disappear out of view behind her.

'Gwydhenn Centre, right?'

'Yeah.'

'Mental.' The driver smirked like he thought he was funny. Not another word was spoken the whole way.

She stepped from car to concrete outside the bleak, sterile entrance of the Gwydhenn Centre and the taxi drove away. Inside she was greeted by a familiar face.

The grumpy woman peered up. 'Gordon Bright?'

'Yes.'

Daphne pushed the internal door and stepped back into the psychiatric hospital, and walked slowly towards where she expected to find Gordon Bright.

Sure enough, there he was, sitting on the same seat at the same table, alone, pulling a large flake of skin from his cheek and placing the disgusting morsel delicately onto his outstretched tongue. This man was as pathetic as he was repulsive. Daphne walked through and slumped down in the seat in front of him, and glared. Gordon Bright looked up at her, and glared back as he swallowed.

A nurse appeared and bent down towards Bright, and said in comforting tones, 'Is everything alright, Gordon?'

He glowered back at her. 'Detective Inspector.'

'Detective Inspector. Sorry, is everything okay, sir?'

Bright's face softened in a fraction of a second, and he smiled. 'Of course, this is my little friend. She's adorable. Look how tiny she is, so diminutive, so... weak.' He smiled and humanity returned to his face. 'I'm joking! She's my adorable little friend.'

The nurse smiled. 'Okay, if you're sure.' She walked away.

Daphne just stared through her hate, daggers pouring through her eyes at him. Every time she tried to speak, raw emotion grabbed her words from her.

'Tongue problems?' asked Bright. 'Cat got your tongue? Or did a tongue get you? When I used to see a woman, I used to see a tongue and do what was necessary to receive it. That was all those police bitches were good for. But now, I don't care for that. Your tongue does not interest me. Only the tentacle tongues are worth my time.'

'Right,' Daphne pushed out with venom. 'The tongue demon. That was yours, wasn't it? The one who got you.'

'We had each other. As we will again.'

Daphne almost smiled. She'd keep the news that she'd dispatched that demon until it would hurt the most. God, she wanted to hurt him. 'You tricked me. You sent me to the washerwoman, and I fell for it. And now a child is dead.'

Bright raised his hand to his mouth and wiggled his fingers, mockingly feigning disgust. 'Oops,' he said, a millisecond before his mouth turned upwards into a smile.

'I'm going to make you pay.'

'Unlikely. He is all-powerful. And our time together was, shall we say, special? Something, shall we say, rubbed off on me. And now I am special too. As close to perfect as a human being can be, do you not see?'

She did not. But she did need help. She hated that she needed help from him.

'I have a question,' said Daphne.

Bright replied in a mocking Scottish accent that sounded eerily like the voice of the bean-nighe. 'A question for a question.'

Fuck you. She thought it, but she did not say it. Not yet. She needed answers before she started throwing too many insults, and ideally very soon, punches.

'I need your help, Gordon, Detective Inspector.'

'Cut that crap, little antling. What wants you? And don't say you want to lick me.'

'The child. A demon has got him. He's possessed.' Daphne felt sadness rise inside. 'I need to know how to stop it, to save the child. Is there any part of you in there that wants to help me? He's a kid for god's sake. He's two.'

'You speak of God. Interesting.'

'Help me. Please. No games, no tricks, no nothing but maybe a sliver of hope at some redemption for you.'

Gordon Bright leaned back and somehow looked taller. 'Redemption? I do not need redemption, little ant. He has already saved me. Saved me from the mundane life of a worm, a pathetic human. My life was worthless before he came, until we shared the vast space inside my little human head. Worthless. And then, when he was with me, it was exhilarating. Everything aligned. It was beautiful. And I will do anything to protect him. Not that he needs my protecting. He is excellent in every way.'

He's gone, actually, I destroyed him.

Gordon Bright leaned forward. 'If it is the fish hook child from the news, good.' He dragged out that last word, dropping it in pitch, so slimy. 'If he is inside the child now, then that would be better for all of us. Especially the child. He is lucky, and I would kill him to get my master back. I owe everything to him. Everything. Is that clear?'

It wasn't clear. What kind of person had Bright become? From high-ranking police officer to this vile mess. He really was a victim, however disgusting he now was.

'No, it's not clear.'

'You have the intelligence of a turd on a twig, Daphne ant. Allow me to spell it out. If he is in the fish hook child, then the fish hook child's life will be sustained and returned. It is a power they have. How else would the little girl they called Pengilly have survived for two years alone? Think, Daphne ant, think if your tiny mind allows it. So it is good for the fish hook child, and it is good for me, because they will break you with him, and we will win.' Bright's hand shook with excitement as he slowly peeled off some more skin and placed the inch long flake into his mouth.

'What did he do to you, Gordon?' Daphne felt no sympathy, and constantly getting called an ant was starting to piss her off.

'He helped me to speak my truth. To say what I really think. What I believe. To be me, Gordon Bright, the man I was meant to be. A true alpha.'

'You were not this man before he got you,' said Daphne.

'Oh, I was.' Bright smiled back. 'I was just lacking the balls to live it. And now, here I am, balls swinging, king of this little colony, awaiting his return to take me out of here, to return to living bliss. Do you want to lick my balls, Daphne ant?'

Daphne didn't take the bait. 'He won't be doing that, Gordon.'

'Oh, he will,' smiled Bright. 'And I will reign over more than just a few nutters in this lowly nutter sanctuary.'

'And if he doesn't?'

'Then I still have the memories of our time, and that is something that no one can take from me. The memories alone are as good as being a king. King worm is better than the lowliest of ant, do you not think? The memory alone, the mere knowledge that we were one... it's... it's ecstasy.'

'How do I beat him?'

'You do not.'

'And what if I already did?'

Gordon Bright paused. And then laughed. And laughed and laughed, laughing so hard he drew the attention of almost everyone in the room, leaning back on his chair and almost falling off with the guttural guffaws that came from deep inside. He managed three words through his howls and roars. 'Beat him? You?' And then his laughter raised in pitch and volume, each slap of his hands on the table angering Daphne more and more.

This was hopeless. This man was truly disgusting, and probably always was, even before the demon had got him. A waste of her time and energy.

Daphne stood. 'I did. He's gone. See ya, Gordon,' she said with dead seriousness, and the laughs were wiped from Bright's face, and he just stared at her, mouth wide open as she backed away.

Bright's smile returned and his eyes moved to Daphne's hands. 'Is that how you hurt your hands? By punching my demon? I find that unlikely, Daphne ant. It looks like wounds of self-hatred to me.' Bright leaned forward and beamed. 'So it seems not only does everyone in the world hate you, but you also hate yourself. Good for you.'

Gordon Bright. She despised him.

She stormed back up the corridor and left the building, threw her lanyard back at the grump, marched across the car park to the taxi rank and got in a cab.

'Hanging Hill Lane, please,' she said. The driver looked over his shoulder and smiled.

As she stared at the smiling man, the realisation hit her. Her last chance had just failed her. Given her nothing. Nothing at all.

She sat in the back seat and watched the world go by, the familiar sights she had grown up with, the streets and her first school, the Old Gallows pub where she had met kind and gentle Paulie, who she was starting to long for more than ever whenever she had a moment to stop and think. The fish and chip shop where her mother's lookalike Mrs Legge had served her chips since she was a child, and which she had occasionally wandered up to in the years since her death, just to get a glimpse of Mrs Legge, the closest thing she could do to pretend to herself she was getting another look at her dear mother. From a certain angle, if the light was dim, they'd look similar enough for Daphne to pretend to herself that she was there, her mother, alive and well, and the pain would ease for just a moment. Now she could see that for the desperation it was. Mrs Legge was a vague lookalike from a certain angle; her mother was just dead.

Those times were gone. It was all gone.

With each passing street, she felt it more. Home was starting to feel like danger, and as the taxi progressed, that danger was getting closer. It was time to fight.

She stepped into her house, closed the door and listened, hoping to hear silence, hoping that the coin had stopped and dropped and would finally stop taunting her. No. It was louder now, so much louder, the noise hammering through the house. She raced upstairs and grabbed the coin, clasping it between both palms. She held on for barely a second before pulling her hands away, bleeding friction burns on both palms, the coin still violently spinning, roaring around the table.

'Why?' she yelled at the coin, but the coin just got louder. 'How do I stop you?'

As if on command, the coin suddenly quietened down, though it showed no signs of slowing. The sound was soft and low, almost silent, and was immediately interrupted by a tapping on a window downstairs. The doorbell chimed, then chimed again. It was getting dark. Darkness, the time the piskies came out.

Another doorbell chime.

And again, and the *tap-tap-tappings* got louder.

Maybe she could start by slaughtering the piskies at her front door.

Daphne looked out of her mother's bedroom window, and sure enough, there they were. Dozens of them surrounded their leader in the middle, who appeared to be smoking a cigar. And next to him, Charl, grinning. He was wearing Alfie's mittens.

As Daphne turned to leave the room, she found herself face-to-face with a mannequin. It may have been in her mother's clothing, but it really looked nothing like her. Any hope of bringing her mother back was feeling long gone. Then she strode out of the door and down the stairs.

Daphne walked into the kitchen and surprised herself as she cried a sudden roar as she pulled the largest, meatiest knife from the rack. Her mother's huge butchering machete. She was ready for a fight and she felt it, craved it, her hands shook for the chance to inflict pain on those who had wronged her. Her other faculties dumbed down and fell away as she felt the urge to do nothing but attack, fight, nothing but carve up the piskie pricks outside her front door. Little fucks. Tiny little fucks. And her knives were as sharp as ever.

A rustle. Outside, in her back garden, something moved. She stared out, focused, looking for what it might have been, but all was quiet and still. There was nothing out there.

Nothing at all.

But then it jumped up from below the window in its little scruffy green hat – a laughing piskie, and Daphne's heart jumped out of her chest. And then another alongside it. Then another. Then the first one. There were three piskies out there, jumping up from below her window and laughing through the glass, and they looked like they were having a wonderful time.

Another one clambered over her wall. Then another. And another.

These would do. They were tiny, barely three feet tall, she could take them all out. She pulled off the heavy iron bar from the back door, struggling with the weight that strangely felt far heavier than normal, and turned the key, which seemed to fight with her fingers. There were only a few, she could carve them up and show them she was going to fight. Maybe that was enough to make the rest back off. But by the time she was done with the lock on the back door that seemed to not want to be turned, the back garden was teeming with them, fence to fence, upon the fence even, and in the tree. Too many. She screamed at the piskies through the glass, and they all screamed back with mocking laughter.

It was no good. There were too many, and she was too beaten to go on. If she couldn't go on, then she would go out, swinging the huge knife, and kill the one who deserved it the most, even if the piskies would get her as she did it. She could no longer run anyway, not while Alfie remained inhabited by a demon, she would never go a second without being taunted by the knowledge she'd abandoned him. She couldn't run. Too tired to hide. No, she was going to kill Charl and disappear the easy way. Death by piskie. Twenty didn't feel too young to die.

This was it. Daphne started a slow walk from the kitchen to the front door, the machete so long and Daphne so short that the sharp tip dragged along the floor. And while she walked, she wept. She cried for Alfie and Sara, feeling guilt in every bone in her body. And how her stupid self had killed them. She cried for Paulie, a man who would have to go on with a dead girlfriend who he would no doubt always remember as the psycho bunny boiler who attacked him for no reason. She cried for the young girl she used to be, the girl who had only just rediscovered her knobble, and who deserved better. As she cried, she walked.

She stepped slowly through the hallway, picking up the knife now, hard, high and ready, ready to slaughter as many piskies as she needed to before she reached Charl. They deserved it.

She cried as she looked down at her feet. She was long past caring about her safety or sanity. It was just time to end this now.

She placed her hand on the old door, ready to open it one last time, blade raised high, and she cleared the tears from her face, and breathed in.

Time to die, Charl.

Time to die fighting, Daphne.

She pulled the door open, too miserable, too angry to care what horrors she might see.

And still, the sight of the person looking back at her shook her to the bone, her anger chased away in a second by a fiery-hot stare that burned away everything in Daphne's consciousness but fear and the lonely feeling of being a small, helpless child.

There were no piskies. No cackling laughter.

Instead, inches in front of her, the only living thing on the street, was a woman who had struck terror into Daphne for as long as she could remember. Now the mountain of a woman glowered down at her with eyes that looked ready to destroy her, and could likely engulf her in flames just by looking if that was what she willed.

Daphne lowered the knife, and spoke weakly through her tear-soaked lips that would barely move.

'Hello, Mrs Hunter,' she said to Sara's mother.

Part 2

The other mother

Chapter Nine

'IT WAS SO DARK, so cold I could see my breath. The carnival was about to start, and I felt so proud at the front of the other girls. Even in the freezing cold, my baton felt fine in my fingers, just twirling it felt so natural and easy. I loved it. I was only nine, and the best in the town with the baton. Even better than the older girls. Oh God, I can feel myself smiling. The muscle memory meant I could twirl, throw and catch, it was easy. I could pull off dance moves and twists even in the bitter cold, in the dark, on the march, in the wind. It was so cold I'll never forget it, and the other girls were complaining their fingers wouldn't work properly. I could do it with my eyes closed, even on that freezing evening. This is weird. I haven't talked about this for years. Not even thought about it.' She stared for a moment at the cactus in the window.

'Just ahead of us majorettes in the carnival that year was the Halloween Hell Float, this huge truck made to look like burning fire, with boys standing on and around it dressed as demons, with red face paint and glowing horns on headbands. It had these big plastic bones that looked like they were pushing the wheels around. Standing on the back was Marcus, a big boy who didn't like doing performances, but loved scaring people. He was there because it was like licensed bullying. That's what he was, just a bully. I could see his breath in the cold, could see he regretted being there freezing. God, I can feel my hands shaking, like they're still cold.' She grasped her hands tightly together before continuing.

'The music started from the truck, this band of older boys on top, and Marcus danced lazily, and as the Halloween Hell Float crept forward, it drowned out the instruments from our majorette's band. That really upset me, that was our biggest moment of the year, and some big truck was being so loud. I can still remember the words, the band just kept repeating the same line. They weren't even in tune. We had the better band, and they drowned us out. The people watching in their hats and scarves and gloves didn't seem to care though, and clapped for the Halloween Hell Float, but, you know what? They applauded us, the majorettes even more, even though you couldn't hear our band. Oh God I haven't smiled like this for a long time, sorry.' She looked up. 'When I threw my baton high into the sky, so high it disappeared into the darkness, I felt like I was on top of the world. It fell perfectly back into my hand, of course it did, and I did a spin so fast the ends of the baton, well, you couldn't even see them because it was a bit dark. When I did a spin I saw all the girls, marching and spinning, the Halloween clowns making mischief behind them as we all moved down the packed high street. It was so good!

'Wow. It really was one of my favourite things to do in the whole world. I'd tuned out Marcus. I was in the zone. And there were so many people! The crowd got so big as the carnival went, and up ahead, I saw all my friends from school had come to watch, all wrapped up warm. Wow, it was so cold. They clapped a little for Marcus on the Hell Float, and the boys dressed up as demons, and, oh yeah, there were people dressed as giant spiders there too! My friends clapped and cheered the Hell Float, pretend-screamed at the spiders, and the Hell Float let out a huge *whooshhhhhh* of steam and it looked amazing in the light. What was it the band was singing, oh, "Down down down to the underground, where the..." something something something, I can't remember. Then came my turn to pass them, and the other girls who were marching behind me.

'I'm sorry, I just need a sip of water. One second.' She sipped and cleared her throat. 'I wanted to put on a show for my friends, and threw the baton even higher, so high it disappeared from view. And then a bright light from the Hell Float flashed right in my eyes and I couldn't see a thing. My vision just went white. I tried to grab the baton. And felt nothing.

'Nothing at all.

'And then I turned and saw the stupid thing clatter across the floor behind me. And then turned again, unsure if I should march on or run back and get it. And I saw them laugh. The light blinded me again, I remember that so clearly. My vision came back just in time to see Marcus pointing and laughing, shining a bright spotlight at me, laughing his stupid head off at me as I picked up my baton. Everyone must have seen me, Marcus and his huge light made sure of that. When I got back to the front of the majorettes, I saw my friends. They were laughing at me. Some were cheering on Marcus the demon in the Hell Float. But Marcus the demon just stared back at me, laughing, pointing, looking at my friends to make sure they were laughing at me too. Goading them. They all laughed. I don't know why they all laughed.

'I'm sorry, can you pass the tissues?' She wiped her face. 'Thanks. Yeah, "Down, down, down to the underground, where the dead rise up and they'll pull you down," that was it. "Down that deep and dark and lonely deep dark hole." Just over and over again, round and round, always out of tune. Oh, and Marcus has this stupid fake tattoo of flames coming from his nostrils. It's so silly, really.' She blew her nose.

'I marched the rest of the carnival route, but my fingers felt cold and it was hard. But I wouldn't make a mistake. I had to make sure I didn't do anything that might draw attention to me, so no one would laugh anymore. I did basic twirls. Nothing too good to draw attention. Not so little that people would notice. So I made it back to the end just fine, all the time behind that band, singing the same line over and over again, feeling like... well, little Daphne felt like, well, awful.

'I never picked up a baton again.'

Doctor Bohn sat back in his chair and looked back with sympathy. 'And you think that's why you learned to become invisible? To protect yourself. I wouldn't disagree with that possibility.' He paused thoughtfully. 'And how do you think this is relative, in terms of how you've felt, to how you feel about what just happened to your neighbours? Do you think, perhaps, that the killer didn't get to you because you managed to look, somehow, invisible?'

'No. I don't think so,' said Daphne. 'I think I just got lucky.' Daphne snorted a little cry out of nowhere. 'Shit, sorry.' She put her hand over her mouth. 'I'm so sorry for swearing.'

'Swear if you want to. We're all adults in here and sometimes a word just slips out.'

Daphne smiled. 'Okay.'

'Try again.'

'Swearing?'

'Yes.'

'Shit.' That felt good.

'Make you feel better?'

'A little.'

'Well fuckity swear then, if it helps. "Fuck it" is a very useful phrase, from a psychological perspective, believe it or not. Try it.'

Daphne felt her face tense and harden in shock. 'Fuck it.' Her face muscles softened. 'Fuck it! Wow.'

'Feel good?'

'Yeah. Thank you. Are you sure you don't mind?'

'My office, my world, my rules.'

'Fuck it,' Daphne said with a smile.

Doctor Bohn wore a smart pinstriped grey suit, perfectly tailored. A timepiece hung from his jacket breast pocket, and he wore a large shining wedding ring. The guy looked exactly like you'd expect a psychologist to look, large but smart beard included. All he was lacking to be an accurate caricature of himself was a monocle, although Daphne secretly liked to suspect he kept one in his desk drawer.

'So what scares you more right now then, Daphne? Now that you know it's over. The thought of being laughed at, or the thought that they haven't caught the killer?'

'Definitely being laughed at.'

'Isn't that interesting?'

It was, but not for the reason that Doctor Bohn thought. Sure, the idea of finding laughter more terrifying than a killer was fascinating, but what was far more interesting was that the killer had in fact been caught, and Daphne had sent it back to Hell with a pointy broomstick. She thought she'd better not say that to a psychologist with the power to commit her to an institution, though.

'And aside from being laughed at? What else scares you? Perhaps we can help with that.'

Myself and my powers. The fact that there are real demons out there. The fact that I know bugger all about the huge swathes of darkness in the world, and the fact that this darkness will be coming for me, and probably very soon.

Everything about my life is terrifying. 'Umm. Spiders,' Daphne lied.

'That's not uncommon. Because of the spider costumes at the Halloween carnival, perhaps.'

'Perhaps.'

The two paused. Daphne dried her eyes.

'Anything else? What else scares you? And I know it can be scary even to talk about it. But that's how we stop being scared. I promise no one will laugh at you in here.'

'I might not see my mum again.'

'With all the magic of psychology and therapy in the world, I cannot make that happen. That pain will only start to decline with acceptance, and acceptance will only come with time. We can talk about that if you like.'

Bullshit. She's at home as a mannequin and I'm bringing her back. 'I guess I'll wait.'

'Do you want to talk about your mother?'

'Not now.'

'So, back to the fears. To go through what you've been through, and cope as well as you have, that's incredible for an eighteen-year-old. It's my job to help you feel less scared. What else scares you?'

Daphne had been thinking about this, and knew the answer. 'Authority.'

'Like, what, or who?'

'The police. Soldiers. Teachers, but not teachers anymore because I don't have any.'

'You're scared of authority figures?'

'Yes. I freeze up or want to run. But I can't run, because I'm frozen, which is good because running from the police looks bad, even if you haven't done anything. Not that I have ever needed to. It's just a scenario that's been in my head some nights.'

'And me? Do you consider me an authority figure? Is that why you struggled to speak freely for our first few meetings?'

That hit Daphne strangely hard. 'Yes. Wow. Sorry.'

'One minute, please.' Doctor Bohn left the room, and Daphne looked around his old wooden office, at the old clock on his large wooden desk, at the handwritten certificates on the wood-panelled wall. Yup, he definitely had a monocle in his drawer.

'Fuck.' That felt good. 'Fuckity fuck fuck.' Oh yes. Now she knew why those words so commonly fell from her mother's mouth. She sat back and smiled, wondering why she felt the urge to prod the cactus in the corner, just to see if it hurt.

When Doctor Bohn returned, he was in jeans and a loose-fitting Beach Boys T-shirt. He sat down. 'How about now? Still scary? I'll tell you what, you can skip the fears today if you want. How about we talk about hopes and dreams? Come back to fears next week?'

Daphne caught herself smiling and, incredibly, felt her whole body relax. This psychologist was seriously good, and not at all what she had expected. Her remaining fear of him had left with the suit. She felt a release of tension, of breath, and felt her eyes water and flow. It somehow felt good.

'You know, I just remembered something. About the carnival. When I dropped the baton, when they all laughed at me, something really weird happened. In my head. Except it didn't feel like it was in my head.'

'Go on.'

'It's hard to explain. It was like I was leaving my head. Like my mind was leaving my body and I was watching from the side. Or above. It's hard to put into words. There were bright lights, the memory is blurry.'

'It's called dissociation and you're not the only one for that to happen to, Daphne. It's a very common trauma response.'

Daphne's jaw dropped. She'd repressed that memory for so long thinking she was weird and that something deeply wrong had happened to her.

'It's a normal protective response. To trauma, to nasty situations. Our minds are apt to just up and leave for a bit until the danger goes.'

'Really?' Daphne was flabbergasted.

'Really. Has it happened since?'

Yes, when a demon was licking my face. 'No.'

'If it ever does, just know you are not broken, and come back and see me if you're worried. You're not broken, Daphne.'

Daphne felt ten times lighter than she had done a few minutes before.

'You're not broken.'

And lighter still, and a few tears pushed through her eyes and crawled down her cheek.

'Okay, Doctor Bohn,' she said through her tears. 'I'll tell you now. My hopes, my dreams and my deep, dark fears.'

Chapter Ten

SARA'S MOTHER STOOD IN Daphne's doorway with a wet-eyed glare that could kill.

Agatha Hunter was a large woman in both height and shoulder mass and towered over Daphne by plenty more than a full foot. She looked upset as any grieving mother would, but more than that, she looked furious. Daphne looked back at her, mouth open, mind and tongue searching for a suitable sound. When she found one, the word slipped out as barely a whisper.

'Sorry.' The sight of her eyes and the realisation that they looked exactly the same as Sara's somehow made her feel even worse.

The words that returned from Mrs Hunter came back through gritted teeth, obvious sadness manifesting as biting anger. 'You. Get inside.'

Daphne obeyed Sara's mother as she always had done ever since she was a little girl. She turned and walked down her hallway as if on autopilot, her heart pounding in her chest, panic rising into her head. When she looked over her shoulder, Mrs Hunter was a few steps behind her, and behind Mrs Hunter, the front door slammed shut on its own so hard that the whole house seemed to rattle and shake.

'Kitchen,' demanded Mrs Hunter, whose voice bellowed through the house that had otherwise never sounded so silent.

Daphne walked meekly through to the kitchen, as terrified as she was sorry. She'd killed this woman's daughter and grandson through her stupidity. This huge woman had every right to be angry with her. Maybe Daphne wouldn't be going out of this world on her own terms anyway. Maybe it would be on Mrs Hunter's. There would be no hiding under the table, comforted by her foot on the knobble now.

'Turn around,' demanded Mrs Hunter, and Daphne turned to face the corner of the room, where she tensed and waited to be struck, perhaps decapitated at the neck, or for the end to come in any way this massive witch wanted her dead. Instead, she heard the squeak of the tap, and water running. A metallic clunk and slide. The soft *whoof* of gas lighting, and then the familiar hiss of the stove. She knew that sequence of sounds. Mrs Hunter was boiling the kettle, and Daphne cried at the thought of the impending scalding as she heard the water begin to bubble, fearing a cascade of boiling water on her head or in her face or just thrown all over her trembling body. She'd be scarred for life. As if life was going to last longer than a few hours anyway. The loud whistle of the kettle signalled her impending agony, and she stood helpless, obeying the woman as always. The hiss of the gas stopped, and Mrs Hunter said, 'My grandson is infected with a demon because of your stupidity.'

Daphne braced for the pain. It wasn't just her daughter she had lost her. Her grandson, her whole lineage, gone through Daphne's mistakes. Poor little Alfie. Maybe the scalding water would wash away the guilt of what she had done. Daphne squeezed her eyes shut and fought the building urge to blub. She would show strength if she could. This was her last chance to make herself proud.

But then, more familiar sounds followed. The *clink* of teacups. Saucers. The *swish* and *pop* the tea caddy made when the lid was pulled off. An ever so soft and light *dink*, the familiar sound of the teabag landing in the pot.

The sound of the fridge opening, and the milk sliding out. Mrs Hunter was making tea. Daphne stifled her tears of relief, and a sob finally came out.

'Silence!' bellowed Mrs Hunter. And then, more calmly, 'You have done untold damage and I have to work fast.'

Work fast: work alone. *She's getting me out of the way. Probably for the best. It would be easy for Mrs Hunter, a proper witch, that way. Fuck. Help. There's no one to help.* Daphne stood as silently as she could and felt seven years old.

Tink. A teaspoon landed in a mug. And then the sound of footsteps heading away towards the kitchen door. Daphne looked up to see Mrs Hunter carrying a tray of teacups out of the kitchen and through the dim hallway, then turn to step up the stairs. Daphne followed and watched as Mrs Hunter carried the tray into her mother's room.

Daphne followed up the stairs, instinctively stepping over the second step – that creak would draw attention to her. When she got to her mother's doorway, she looked in through the open door.

Mrs Hunter was standing in front of the row of mannequins dressed in her old friends' clothes with the tray of tea. With a body as utterly still as the mannequins themselves, she twisted her neck and head, and glowered at Daphne. 'Unconventional. Might just work. I'll deal with you later.' And then the bedroom door slammed shut with such force that the whole wall buckled and bounced in front of her.

As Daphne's eyes fell on the wooden door, it felt like every muscle in her body was shaking. Of all she had faced in her life, the demons, the deaths, the piskies chasing her through the woods, it was Mrs Hunter, right now, that was somehow the most terrifying.

Daphne considered running out of the house and never coming back. Maybe now was the time after all, the time to walk up the hill towards an imagined new paradise, and keep going until she got there. Mrs Hunter could deal with the demons. Mrs Hunter could save Alfie.

No. This was her fault, her doing, and her responsibility to fix. If Agatha Hunter didn't rip all her limbs off first.

Chapter Eleven

DAPHNE SAT AT HER bedroom desk, watching the coin go round and round, migrating across the surface one way, then the other, as the metal spun and whirred. Its initial use, to force her into a decision, was now long outdated. Now it was whirring all by itself, perhaps trying to convey a message. Perhaps telling her not to give up. Perhaps telling her to wait for a third option. Whatever, her old plan didn't matter now. As soon as Agatha Hunter had arrived, everything had changed. Now, just maybe, there was a chance to save Alfie.

And still... those demons, the bean-nighe, Charl and the piskies, Gordon Bright... she couldn't get them out of her head. She wanted to kill them all. They deserved it.

It happened as fast as a crack of a whip. One second Daphne was staring into space, fighting her tiredness. A blink later, and she didn't know if she'd dozed off and then awoken, or if the huge woman really was that fast.

Agatha Hunter stood in the doorway, the top of her head barely under the wood of the frame. She looked at the coin. 'Making a decision, I see. I think it's best I make that one for you.' She walked forwards to Daphne, put her hands on her massive knees and put her head eye to eye, and Daphne felt dread build inside her. 'Now,' continued Mrs Hunter, 'I am going to be back, and I am going to put you through insufferable pain. On that, you can count. But first, I have things to do. So in the meantime, sleep.'

Daphne's world went black as she immediately drowned in a magnetic sleep that pulled her down.

When she awoke, all was dark.

✳ ✳ ✳ ✳ ✳

The clock struck ten. It took a while for Daphne's grogginess to fade and her situation to return to her. At that point, she wished she'd just stayed asleep. No longer was she just up against three demons and an army of piskies. Now there was a furious and powerful witch, the mother and grandmother of those she had killed.

'I'm fucked,' she said as the world inside her head started to come back alive. She looked at the coin, still spinning as fast as the moment it had left her finger and thumb. 'Stop!' she shouted at it. 'Stop you fucker!' It just kept spinning. As anger rose, she swiped the coin off the desk and hard into the wall. The coin bounced back and hit her smack in the face, stinging her nose, and bounced down onto the desk where it continued to spin and slowly make circles around the surface. 'Fuck!'

Breathe and be clever.

If Mrs Hunter wasn't going to kill her, she'd have to prove she was worth keeping alive. That she could be of use in saving her grandson.

She grabbed her laptop and loaded up the social media sites and searched the normal useful terms. WTF. Weird. Nothing useful came up. Mostly posts about the death of the celebrities on the yachts.

She ran downstairs and turned on the news, expecting it to be just as useless. It wasn't. The report showed CCTV footage of a very young boy walking through the deserted town centre late at night, naked, his bum blurred out digitally. Police were searching for the boy and had found nothing. A still image from a different camera showed him smashing a window of a fancy dress shop. Another camera showed an image of the boy – Alfie, it was definitely and now clearly Alfie – walking away from the shop fully clothed. The image was black and white and blurry, but the strange attire appeared to be some kind of uniform. He walked like a fully grown adult, not the stumbling gait of a two-year-old.

Perhaps Daphne could still be useful. Perhaps she could still put things right, if just a little.

If she could put this right, maybe the pain would go away, if just a little.

Just a little. That would do. She would head into town where Alfie was last seen.

So she grabbed her coat and keys and stormed to the front door. She had no plan. She didn't care. Her plans had caused this. She was going to wing it all the way to end.

When she opened the door, she gasped and stepped backwards. Agatha Hunter towered above her in the doorway, floating towards her six inches above the ground, a terrifying look on her contorting face. With a swing of Agatha's huge hand, Daphne flew back down the hallway and onto the floor. She was a good foot or two from making contact, but Daphne's face rung like it had been hit by a sledge hammer. Agatha Hunter wasn't letting her go anywhere. She was being punished. Number Two Hanging Hill Lane was now her prison.

Her anger felt utterly pointless with her judge, jury and executioner standing at the front door keeping her inside. *Executioner*. Shit. That didn't sound good. Agatha Hunter didn't look in the mood to give anyone a peaceful death. This was going to be horrible. This was going to hurt. Still, those fish hooks must have hurt, too. Daphne ran into the kitchen, closed the door, and hid.

All went quiet.

The coin continued its soft and distant whirr around the desk upstairs. It taunted her.

Hopeless.

Helpless.

Lost.

All the feelings swirled around Daphne's head and body. She was on the edge. The edge of a breaking mind. Then, if Agatha Hunter hadn't finished her off, the demons would have a way in. She had to get rid of those feelings. The old tricks, a bath or warm shower, a comedy TV show or a phone call with a friend were suddenly so inadequate. She needed something stronger. Anything stronger, consequences be damned.

That's how she found herself standing on a wooden stool in the kitchen looking through the old ornate spice rack. The love salts were definitely a way to make things feel better. A bit of warmth. A bit of love. Maybe even a sprinkling of forgiveness. It sounded divine. But what else was there on the rack?

Sleepy Green Spice. That one sounded interesting. Devil's Fungus. Oh no, that one looked horrible. Daphne took the pot from the rack and looked through the glass. Inside were small fingernail-sized pieces of wrinkly dried meat. They looked disgusting. Devil's Fungus? Surely not actual devil meat? That would be absurd. But then, it still kind of fitted. She'd never looked on this rack before aside from grabbing the love salt. Heaven's Splinter. *Ooooh*.

She considered the love salts. A sure winner for a night off the pain. But Devil's Fungus... that one looked disgusting but intriguing. And then, stepping down with the pots in hand, she caught her reflection in the window. She looked just like her mother. That was enough for her to stop this. She set the pots down and, at a complete loss about what to do, decided to revert to her old comforts and have a nice warm shower. It wasn't as comforting as it used to be, not since a demon had used a horror movie-esque shower moment to terrify her two years before. But if she was going to be in a prison, she may as well enjoy the facilities.

Shower time. A moment of peace. Finally.

She walked upstairs, chucked her clothes on the floor, grabbed a towel and walked back down to the shower. The spray came out as warm and strong as always. If only it had felt as good, if only the water could have washed away just an ounce of guilt, just a bit of the stench of the bean-nighe that seemed to cling to her. When she turned off the tap, she felt just as tired as she had done when she'd stepped in. The scabs on her knees had opened and stung.

The last drops of water pattered on the bathtub floor, and Daphne pulled back the curtain. She jumped back, screaming, her hands across her chest, backing into the corner against the cold tiles.

In the middle of her bathroom, sitting on a chair in his tailored pinstriped suit, one leg crossed over the other revealing long socks under the slightly-too-short trousers, Doctor Bohn looked back at her, twisting the end of his beard, smiling.

Chapter Twelve

DOCTOR BOHN LOOKED EXACTLY as he always had done, upright with perfect posture, tall with a perfectly groomed beard, his polished timepiece hanging from his jacket pocket. But something was different. Something wasn't right. He'd never had a grin like that before.

'Ahhh,' came a guttural sound from the man's mouth. The thick, slimy tone was instantly recognisable. A demon. The demons had taken Doctor Bohn. 'We need to talk,' said the demon in the doctor. 'It's time for your... how shall we say it? Therapy? It is time for us to cleanse your mind, rid your head of the shitty part of yourself. Which is, of course, all of you.'

Daphne trembled, naked, with nowhere to go. The unfairness of the demon tactics, the injustice of it all. They knew just how to get to her.

'Worry not, Daphne ant. I'm not here to hurt you. I'm a doctor, remember?'

Daphne stared back with nothing to say, cornered prey.

The doctor reached forward, grabbed the shower curtain and ripped at it, and it came falling down and lay on the wet floor by the bath. A curtain was no barrier from the demon, but it still somehow felt worse. Now there was nothing between them.

'Do you need a shower partner, Daphne ant? I can cleanse your body too.'

Daphne shook her head and pushed herself back against the cold hard tiled wall.

'I can sanitise your body, make everything go away.' Doctor Bohn stood and stepped forward. 'Do you remember, Daphne, in our sessions? Our discussions? You told the doctor everything. Your deepest, darkest fears, did you not? I think we can have some fun with that.'

Daphne's fight had abandoned her. Without clothes, she had lost a protective part of her.

'For example,' the doctor said, reaching forward with an outstretched finger and running just the very tip across Daphne's soaking wet forearm, 'you say you fear losing your mother forever. Consider it done.' The tall man snapped his fingers. 'She who killed your mother is one you shall soon meet. She is excited to meet you. She has been watching for a long time.'

Daphne snapped back. 'I killed your friend and I will kill you next.'

The demon in Doctor Bohn smiled through the doctor's beard. 'You killed no one. And what you did, you did not do to any friend of mine. You weeded out the weak of us. Now, you are presented with the strong. It is now just up to us to decide who will command you. The fungus always gets its ant. History has shown that forever.'

Daphne's eyes darted around the room, looking for something, anything, a weapon, an escape. There was nothing.

'Remember when you told me,' said the doctor's voice, 'that you hate hugs? That you dread the moment that someone will demand an affectionate squeeze? Well let's start easy shall we.' He smiled. 'Come here, naked Daphne ant. Give the doctor a cuddle. The doctor will squeeze you now.'

'No.' It was all she could muster.

'Well okay. How about this then?' The doctor's arm reached out towards Daphne. As the hand approached her hips, she stepped aside, expecting the outstretched fingers to follow her and grab her naked body. Instead the doctor's arm just kept lengthening, and slowly continued its path until it reached the tap. Long fingers switched the water on, soaking Daphne again. 'Things are about to get hot, Daphne ant. Hot.' The demon then reached for the temperature control, and slowly turned the dial to red. Daphne backed away from the water but couldn't escape it. Steam started to rise from the water as it fell. 'Not as hot as Hell, Daphne, you need not complain.'

'Stop!' she shouted back, swiping her hand at the temperature control, but each time her hand was met by the unnaturally long arm of the smiling doctor, swatting her away, then turning up the temperature some more.

Daphne could see her skin turning red under the water. 'Stop, it hurts!' As she closed her eyes, a vision flashed up of Mrs Hunter scalding her with the kettle.

'These human contraptions don't go very hot, do they? Perhaps I should add a little heat? Bring some from home. Some real fire.'

'No!' shouted Daphne, her skin stinging. 'Please stop it!'

'Ah, the ant finally begs. Your wish is my command, Daphne ant. Now try this.' The demon swung the control the other way, and the cold water hit Daphne hard, pushing against her burned skin. 'I think we can do better,' said the demon in the doctor, and the water flying from the shower froze mid-air, hitting Daphne like shards of sharp hail.

'Stop!'

'Okay,' said the demon. The water and ice stopped. The demon spoke in the doctor's familiar voice. 'You see, Daphne, we have to work through the pain together. That's how therapy works. I bring you pain until you let me in and we are together. Is that clear? Is that understood?'

Daphne stood, shivering, and nodded.

The demon's head jolted up at her. 'So, you will let me in? Or shall I call forth the spiders and guide them as they tunnel into your ear?'

Daphne's head shook before she had a chance to think.

The demon hissed. 'Well then,' said the demon in the doctor, 'I suggest you prepare for some real suffering.' He turned and left the bathroom.

And Daphne was alone and freezing.

So very, very, alone.

Somewhere in the house, Doctor Bohn started singing Daphne's mother's favourite song.

Chapter Thirteen

THE DRY TOWEL FELT like razor blades on Daphne's cut and burned skin as she shivered and covered herself. The bathroom door looked so weak that she wondered how she could fight back against the demon in Doctor Bohn. Nothing around her resembled any kind of weapon; she was in a room full of uselessness. One toothbrush, one hairbrush, herself in the mirror – useless.

But what difference did it make? If the demon had wanted to harm her, really harm her, it could have done. It could have killed her right there in the bath, by drowning, hanging her from the shower pipe, or even just a simple death by beating. It hadn't. She stepped out of the bathroom and looked up and down the hallway, her ears tuning in deeply to the quiet. No one moved in the darkness. She stopped still and listened, held her breath, and heard nothing. Nothing but the soft whirring of the coin upstairs in her bedroom.

She crept towards the stairs, keeping her fast breath as quiet as she could, listening for any sign of the demon somewhere inside her house.

Everything was quiet.

Everything was still.

She stepped onto the stairs. The second creaked and she stopped. And heard nothing more. She walked up slowly and approached her bedroom door, expecting him to pounce at any moment. Expecting some kind of trickery in her bedroom, the room in which she had been terrorised before.

The bedroom door was closed.

She hadn't closed it.

And on the other side of the door, a creak. That familiar sound her desk chair made every time she leaned back.

Daphne didn't open the door, instead turning around and stepping into her mother's room. She could put some clothes on in there, even if they weren't a perfect fit. And there they were: the five mannequins, who didn't look the same as they had last time she had seen them.

Morwenna Rowe's hair now reached her shoulders, and looked as fiery and red as ever. Gugwana's curls were growing too, thick and black, and her lips looked as real as on any human. Daphne studied her mother's mannequin, desperate to see some progress. She was as plastic as ever.

And then she jumped as her heart thudded and tried to break into her throat.

Deanna Tamblyn was looking at her.

The mannequin blinked. Deanna Tamblyn's eyes were completely alive, as human as any other pair of eyes in the world. Daphne stared at the mannequin's wet, brown irises. The eyes stared back as the rest of the face remained as still as a statue.

Daphne glanced at the figure in Sara's clothes. As synthetic as the moment she'd put them on her. And again at Deanna's mannequin. The alive eyes just stared back, and blinked again. And then again. And then they looked to the side.

'You're coming back,' Daphne murmured. 'What changed?' Her toes brushed something on the floor. The tray of teacups. Agatha Hunter had done this. She was bringing them back. 'There's a demon in here,' Daphne said. And the eyes in Deanna's mannequin blinked twice.

Daphne stared at the mannequin with the real eyes, and the eyes stared back. And then the eyes looked sharp right, and a little down, and then back at Daphne. Then blinked again and looked back to the same place. There was information in those eyes. A message.

Daphne looked at the spot where Deanna Tamblyn's eyes were looking. It was halfway up Gugwana's mannequin. Daphne looked at Deanna. The eyes looked back at her, and then again to Gugwana's hip. Where the knife lived.

Daphne stepped to Gugwana's colourfully adorned mannequin, put her hand onto the handle, and looked back at Deanna's eyes. They blinked twice. She took the knife out, and looked again. They blinked once more, and looked the other way. Towards Daphne's room.

Daphne was being told there was a demon in the room, and to destroy it.

Perhaps the demon in Doctor Bohn wasn't expecting her to open the door and pounce with a ready blade. It might just work, though the innocent doctor would die too. The eyes blinked again, and looked again at her bedroom door. At Daphne. At the knife. At the door. She was being sent to kill the demon.

She had surprise on her side.

But the doc would die.

And if she didn't do it? The lovely Doctor Bohn would die anyway.

The eyes continued the triangle. Daphne's eyes, the knife, her bedroom.

'Okay,' Daphne let out in a soft breath. She quietly opened her mother's wardrobe and took out the most practical thing she could find. If she was going to be found dead in crazy circumstances, she at least wanted to be wearing clothes. Though the fact that they were clearly her mother's would, to any investigating officer finding her body in the days to come, only make the circumstances look even more bizarre.

The old dress was a little loose fitting, so she grabbed the cord from her mother's dressing gown still hanging on the wall, and tightened it around her waist. The Daphne in the mirror looked back at her. The fashion student in her recognised immediately how ridiculous it looked. And just how much like her mother she looked in the dress. There wasn't time to think about such things. Doctor Bohn was in her room, and inside Doctor Bohn, a demon.

She crept to her bedroom door, gripping Gugwana's knife tightly in her right hand, her left on the handle. In one moment, she could throw the door open and leap in. She checked the ill-fitting clothes to be sure she could move freely even in a stabbing motion, then slashing, and stab and slash she could, and prepared herself to throw open the door, to pounce, and to strike.

The chair inside the room creaked again. She knew exactly where the demon was in the room. It could be done in a flash. In one movement. She looked through her mother's open doorway, where Deanna Tamblyn's mannequin was staring at her out the corner of its eyes, blinking, blinking, double-blinks, faster and faster.

She took a long, silent breath, and raised her right hand into the position to strike.

She slammed the handle down, threw the door open, and pounced, flying into the room, and engaged her arm muscles to stab straight into the head of the demon in the doctor.

She stopped just in time. And fell back. And burst into tears.

The room smelled strongly of lavender, like the house hadn't smelled for over two years.

Sitting on her desk chair in the dark shadows of her room, hunched over the coin that spun on the desk, in the way that only one person hunched, was not the doctor. The silhouetted figure was a woman, sitting at a certain angle in the dim light, her clothes familiar, her hat once a birthday gift from Daphne. She didn't even look up as she spoke.

'Hello again,' said Martha Locke, Daphne's mother.

Chapter Fourteen

DAPHNE DROPPED THE KNIFE and flew forward as her mother turned towards her, and buried her head into her shoulder as a flood of emotion cascaded through her. She could barely breathe as tears poured from her eyes and her mother's arms squeezed her back, and Daphne couldn't bear to look, to see the woman she had missed so, so much. The gut-punch somehow both hurt and was one of the best moments of her life.

She even smelled the same, the detergent in her clothes she had always used, the strong lavender perfume, although there was another smell too. The underlying smell of fish and chips.

Daphne squeezed her eyes shut, pushing some water out, and dried them on her mother's blouse, one she knew so well. Then she leaned back to finally take a good look at the woman she had missed with all of her heart and soul for so long now, to finally see again the face that she had dreamed about almost every night, to finally take in the moment, the re-connection, the relief and joy.

And her jaw dropped.

And her heart broke all over again.

How could a heart so broken still beat so fast?

She looked so much like her. The woman had the same mannerisms, the same bags under her eyes, the same grey-ing hair and was wearing her clothes. But the ever-caring look in her eyes wasn't there. The nose was a little different, flatter. No mole on the chin.

For a moment, Daphne refused to believe it. Her head shook by itself. She wanted to believe it was her mother so, so much, and any other truth was too painful to bear. And yet, she had to bear it.

The woman smiled, and a low, guttural yet sibilant voice shot from her mouth.

'Gotcha again, stupid.'

Daphne fell back against the wall and sobbed so hard her face felt like it was ready to burst. The woman followed her, then bent down and picked up the knife.

The demon inside the woman in Daphne's mother's clothes grinned. 'Need a hug from Mamma?'

And suddenly it made sense. The smell of chip fat. The demon had taken Mrs Legge from the local takeaway. The woman who looked so like her mother that Daphne had been sneaking peeks to feel close to her.

'You're not Mum,' spat Daphne.

'I think we established that already, stupid. Keep up. And yet you see nothing else, am I right?'

The demon was very right.

'Now,' continued the demon. 'There is someone I wish you to meet. She is going to become someone very important to you. As important as your real mother was, you see, and, your mother is never coming back. She's gone. Dead. Rotting in a river.'

Daphne couldn't help but believe it.

'And yet,' it continued, 'I am the one who gets to play in your mummy suit. I get to walk around dressed as your pathetic mother, and do all sorts of disgusting things. You can watch if you like. Would you like to watch, daughter?'

'You are disgusting.'

'Oh, I know. It's this pig-ugly face. There are people who have not heard of your mother's humorous passing. They will see and they will talk. "I saw Martha Locke pissing in the park with her dress up around her titties," they will say. "Martha Locke has become quite the whore," they will gossip.'

Daphne glanced at the knife, now out of reach. The demons had given her the illusion of returning to her everything that was important, and whipped it away a second later. Just when she thought her heart couldn't be any more broken, they'd smashed it again. If they needed to break her heart to possess her, she knew they had done it, even if the feeling was now masked by rising rage.

'You won't win,' she said. 'You can't win. I. Will. Not. Break.' Daphne spat in the face of the demon in the woman-skin and instantly felt terrible as her saliva dripped down the face of the woman who looked too much like her mother. She didn't let on. If any demon was going to take her, it wouldn't be this fucker. This was the most evil one of all. That trick truly hurt the most. Daphne looked at the door. She could still make a run for it. Find Olivia. Come back and kill the demon inside Mrs Legge. Kill the demon inside Doctor Bohn. But the demon in Mrs Legge just laughed as she lifted Daphne from the floor with one hand and threw her hard against the window.

'You will not run anywhere, diminutive daughter.' In the back garden, piskies crowded. Standing on the back wall, was Charl. Charl looked at Mrs Legge and waved, and laughed. 'See. Where will you run?'

Charl cackled.

Charl has to suffer.

And yet, Daphne had nothing. No way out or through. Her clothes still felt like they scraped along her burned-red skin.

'There's someone you must meet,' said the demon.

'I know the piskie,' Daphne replied. 'I'm going to make him pay.'

The demon just laughed. 'No, my dear. Behind you.'

Daphne shot around.

Standing on the floor in front of her, barely two feet tall, dressed in the uniform of a high-ranking British soldier from World War Two complete with ceremonial baton, was Alfie.

The child, or the demon inside the child, took three steps towards Daphne and looked up at her. Alfie looked just like he always had done, aside from the evil grin and army costume. Just as Daphne thought that nothing in the world could hurt as much as being fooled into thinking her mother was alive, the demons had found something that did.

Alfie was possessed.

'I'll leave you two to it,' said the demon inside Mrs Legge. 'You've got some talking to do.' Mrs Legge's face looked at Daphne and softened in exactly the way that her mother's used to, and she felt her heart break one more time. 'I'll put the supper on.'

Her mum used to say that just like that, with that expression.

And then Mrs Legge walked out the door, turning as she did. 'Do as he says, listen to your mother. Me, that is, not the one I killed and threw in the river.'

It was that demon. The demon in Mrs Legge that killed her mother. Daphne felt utter hatred flow in.

Alfie hit the baton on the palm of his hand.

It spoke with a strange two-toned voice, the high pitch voice of a human child accompanied by an unnaturally low growl, the two notes unnervingly discordant, always together on every syllable the demon in the child spoke. 'Let me in, ant. It's over.'

Through the hatred, the final hope in Daphne's world collapsed in, and she knew the demon was right.

Chapter Fifteen

DAPHNE LOOKED OUT OF her bedroom window. She didn't really care what was out there, even if it was dozens of piskies, cackling and dancing in her back garden. She just had to look somewhere else. Anywhere else but at Alfie, possessed by a demon, because of her.

'Careful now,' said the demon. 'They bite.'

Daphne continued to stare. Charl was climbing a tree, effortlessly, branch by branch, higher and higher. Daphne's eyes flicked across the window. The latch was fastened shut. As long as the demon didn't open it, Charl wasn't getting in, even if he did make the impossibly long jump from tree to window.

'Oh, he's putting on a show,' said the demon inside Alfie. The child moved the desk chair, climbed up on it, and stared outside. Daphne felt him there. She didn't look. Couldn't look.

Charl reached the highest branch that looked thick enough to take his weight, and looked at Daphne. Daphne looked back. And then Charl turned around, dropped his trousers and bent over, revealing everything to Daphne as the whole garden full of piskies erupted in cackling laughter.

And still Daphne did not look away. Anything was better than looking at Alfie as a possessed child. She just stared unblinking at Charl's tiny arse and miniature balls. Her rage had long peaked. If she ever got her hands on him, she would rip those little balls off and the rest of him to pieces. That wasn't feeling very likely right now.

'Look at me.' Said Alfie's voice.

She didn't.

'Look at me,' it said again.

She didn't.

Whack! The baton smashed Daphne's knuckles so hard it drew blood, and pain seared through her whole body. She'd never felt bodily pain like it, and as she bent double, gripping her throbbing knuckles, she finally looked up at the demon in the suit of Alfie.

'Oh baby, baby,' said the demon. 'What are those words?'

Daphne glared back, her mind not even thinking to answer the question.

The demon child answered it for her. 'Hit me, baby.'

Whack!

Daphne grabbed her hand again, and blood dripped from it.

'One more time?'

Whack! Right on the elbow bone.

Daphne finally spoke, anger and pain shooting out in her voice. 'Why do you shits always come with stupid fucking sticks?'

The child smiled, jumped down from the chair, and looked straight at Daphne.

'Because, my little orphan friend, it is simply because it is the thing of which you are most scared.'

Anger rose at those words. She wasn't scared of stupid sticks.

She was trapped. The demon was in the human shield of Alfie Hunter, her best friend's child, and she couldn't touch it. She was being tortured by yet another hitty-stick and her mother's dead ringer dressed in her mother's clothing using phrases her mother used to use. It was heartbreaking.

And then another phrase echoed up the hallway, in the voice of her beloved mother.

'Daphne!' came the yell. 'Come on down for supper.'

Alfie looked up at Daphne and smiled. 'Oh good. Dinner time. I was getting hungry. Chop chop.'

Chapter Sixteen

THE DEMON IN ALFIE'S body prodded Daphne out of her room using the stick as an incentive to hurry, and she walked with wobbly legs down the stairs. The second step from the bottom creaked its familiar creak. And then a *clink* came from inside the lounge.

'Faster,' came the little voice from behind Daphne, and she walked to the lounge doorway. Inside, the dinner table was laid with the tablecloth her mother only ever used for special occasions. The fancy china was out. The posh wine glasses. Around the table, two of the four chairs were occupied. The demon-possessed bodies of Mrs Legge and Doctor Bohn sat at two edges, a tall stool at another, and a vacant chair waited in Daphne's habitual eating spot. Daphne stepped into the lounge, and a long tentacle slipped out from the bottom of Mrs Legge and pushed the chair towards her.

'Sit,' said the figure who looked upsettingly like her mother. It was a heartbreaking sight, seeing this woman dressed in her mother's clothes sitting at her mother's spot at the dinner table. Daphne was stunned, fixed into place at the threshold of the lounge, until a whack on the back of her legs made her step forward again towards her chair. Little Alfie ran around to the other side and sat opposite. Daphne stopped by her chair, and the three familiar faces all stared at her.

The kind therapist. Her friend's two-year-old dead son. Her own mother's doppelganger. All staring at her as if they were completely innocent and this was entirely normal.

'Sit,' commanded Doctor Bohn.

'Sit,' said Alfie with a cheeky smile that looked like the kid could have been his completely normal self, reminding Daphne of the funny cute kid Alfie was.

'Sit down, daughter.'

Daphne didn't want to sit. She wanted to run. And then she smelled smoke.

'Oh shit, it's burning,' said Mrs Legge. It was a phrase that had made Daphne laugh countless times as a young teenager. There was no laughter this time as Mrs Legge got up and left the room.

Alfie stared at Daphne. 'Sit.'

Doctor Bohn stared too. 'Sit.'

'And if I don't?'

Doctor Bohn looked at her with a deadly serious expression. 'Then all hell will rain down on you and everyone you know.'

Daphne sat. She didn't want to. And yet she knew if she didn't, she would be hurt. If she tried to run, she would be punished. If she tried to fight, she would be overpowered and beaten. So she sat, and Mrs Legge returned with a huge tray of food, and placed it in the middle of the table. The tray that her mother had only ever used on special occasions. The woman posing as her mother picked up the serving spoon and started to move potatoes onto the plates. They were roasted. A puff-pastry pie waited, ready to be cut, steam seeping through a slit in the perfect- ly browned top. A gravy boat harboured a thick, glossy liquid. The demon inside Mrs Legge had made a roast. She served up as the rest sat in silence, all eyes glaring at Daphne. Then Mrs Legge took her seat, and spoke.

'We have been thinking, Daphne ant. About which one of us shall take you. And we have decided.'

'None of you,' said Daphne. 'You can't hurt me. You can't kill me. You need me. And while you need me, I know you can't kill me.'

'No,' said Mrs Legge. 'We need nothing but a head.'

'That's not true,' said Daphne, hoping she was correct.

Alfie hissed. Doctor Bohn rose from his seat. He was a tall, thin man, and made the distance to Daphne in one large pace. He crouched, and studied her face. Daphne stared back, defiant on the outside, desperately controlling her urge to shake and scream. And wretch. Doctor Bohn absolutely stank, the now familiar stench of a demon. Then Doctor Bohn reached into his inside jacket pocket and pulled out a small metal ring on the end of a chain. Inside the ring was curved glass. He rested it in his right eye. A monocle. The doctor really did have a monocle. He studied Daphne's chin, her mouth, her cheek, squeezing her flesh with his finger and thumb as he looked through the thick lens. And then he looked into her eye.

Daphne stared back at the demon doctor, and inside that small circle of glass held between the man's finger and thumb, inside the doctor's eye that had blown up and distorted in the magnification of the old eye glass, she could see everything. The horned, scaled beast. The fiery hell in which it lived. Flames of colours she had never before seen. The moment the beast had taken Doctor Bohn played out as though on a miniature screen inside the glass. She looked closer, and she knew.

'It wasn't you,' she said.

Surprise flickered over the face of Doctor Bohn. 'What wasn't me, ant?'

'Who killed my mother. It wasn't you.' She turned to Alfie and Mrs Legge. 'Which one of you was it? Which one of you killed her?'

Alfie and Mrs Legge looked at each other. And then they laughed. They laughed and laughed and laughed so hard. Doctor Bohn slumped back to his seat laughing with them, each bellow infuriating Daphne even more. Eventually, when the laughter had died down enough to speak, Mrs Legge looked at Daphne.

'You will never know. Until you let us in. And then you will see everything you want to see. Answer all the questions you still have. Feel everything you want to feel. See memories of her like you are really with her. Experience her again. And it would be so easy.'

Mrs Legge picked up a large knife and leaned in. She reached forwards and cut the pie evenly into four pieces. She stood, and walked around the table, sliding a quarter of the pie onto each plate. It was exactly the serving technique her mother had used. 'Experience your mother's cooking, her bedtime stories, her silly words.'

Daphne stared at the woman as she sat back down, large knife still in hand. She hated that she was starting to see the appeal. But there was no chance she was going to accept. She had to fight back, to show them she would not be beaten. 'You've lost, haven't you?' she said. 'Your normal tactics, the scaring, the torture, the hitting and licking. All failed. You didn't win. So now you're desperate, so desperate you've made me bloody dinner. Because you've lost.'

'Not so,' said Mrs Legge.

'Oh no? Then tell me, how many witches have you had to make dinner for to possess? Or are you desperate?'

And again, the three possessed all fell about laughing.

'Alice Turner, 1223,' said Mrs Legge, laughing harder.

'Elizabeth Tarr, 1225,' said Doctor Bohn, reaching for a knife.

'Audrey May, 1226,' said Alfie, his little shoulders bouncing with laughter.

'Jane Jones, 1226,' said Mrs Legge.

And on they went. Name after name, year after year, until Daphne snapped and shouted.

'Enough! You have made your point.'

'We know,' said Alfie, popping a huge chunk of pie into his mouth. 'Piskies are tender today. Eat.'

There was no way Daphne was going to eat, although she wasn't at all upset that this might be piskie on the plate. Hopefully it would be Charl. Charl in the pie. No, not Charl. She wanted to get him herself.

'We are not here to persuade you, to tempt you,' said Mrs Legge. 'We know you will break when we tell you to, which will happen imminently.'

Doctor Bohn swallowed and cut into his pie. 'We are here to sustain these pathetic worm bodies first, and thought it would be interesting to see how Daphne Locke, the most stupid witch in town, would react. And so far, you have not disappointed.'

'Fuck you all,' Daphne said. The words felt somehow weird. Somewhere deep in her brain she still saw Mrs Legge as her mother, and felt bad for saying that, even though her mother used to swear like a trooper.

'No,' said Doctor Bohn. 'Okay, here it is. Here is the truth. We have been watching you. We have learned what we need to know. And finally, we will all agree on the next turn of events.'

'I doubt it.'

'Oh I know it. So, now is the time. Here is what we will do. We will make sure you are unable to move, yet able to think and see clearly. You already know that will be easy for us, yes, Daphne ant?'

Daphne silently held her poker face.

The doctor reached across the table and picked up the large knife. 'I think we all know that will be not difficult. And then, we use this blade. Isn't it a thing of wonder, how after all these years, it still cuts so easily, as if by magic?'

He was right, and Daphne shook at the thought of where this was going.

Doctor Bohn looked at Alfie. 'And then the child will take this blade, and saw pieces of itself off until the little shit dies, permanently this time.'

Daphne stared back, utterly horrified. She believed every word. And then she felt something wet, slimy, move across her back, then her shoulders and arms, squeezing her to the back of her chair.

Mrs Legge stood, and long scaley arms faded from nothing into solid view, long, long fingers fully wrapping around Daphne, trapping her and squeezing her to her chair.

Mrs Legge smiled excitedly. 'And then, you, Daphne ant, broken and bleeding, will leave your head, for our friend inside the child to leave him and enter you. That is the only way it will stop. To save the ant-child you call Alfie, you must let her swap places, let the demon inside his head into yours. Is that clear?'

Daphne stared back blankly, desperate for a way to stop this. It was horribly clear.

'Yes?' asked Doctor Bohn. 'Not that we need a yes from you. It would just be nice to know we are clear before we begin.'

Daphne was still and silent as a bone.

'I think that's a yes,' said Mrs Legge.

'Pass the knife then,' said Alfie, still chewing on some piskie.

'Well then,' said Doctor Bohn. 'Shall we get started?'

'Wait!' yelled the demon in Alfie, who stood up on his stool, stepped onto the table and walked across the food, huge knife in hand, knocking over glasses and squashing the pie under a bare foot as he walked. He stopped with a foot on Daphne's plate, looked at the knife, then the prop military baton, smiled, raised the stick high, and slammed it down on Daphne's head. She did her best to hide the pain, but it hurt like a bitch. Alfie then turned around, walked back to his stool, turned and dropped down, and looked up at Daphne. 'I just wanted to test the skull that I'll be living in. It's as thick as I expected.'

'Fine,' said the demon in Doctor Bohn, wiping the corner of his mouth with a napkin. 'If we are now ready, we will begin.'

Chapter Seventeen

THE LITTLE ARM OF Alfie Hunter held the large knife up, his other chubby little arm extended, and the blade of the knife moved in and rested on his shoulder.

'First,' said the demon in the child, 'I shall remove the arm. Then each leg.'

'The pain,' interjected Mrs Legge. 'Don't forget about the pain.'

'Of course,' said Alfie's voice. 'After each cut, I shall retreat a little from the child's consciousness, and let him feel the pain. And he shall show that pain to you. And then I will return to remove the next part of the child, until he is dead.'

'You already killed him,' replied Daphne – a lie and they all knew it, but she had to try something. 'He's already dead, and now you're just parading his body to me.'

'Oh no,' said the demon in the child. 'That is not how this works. I can sustain the life from within for as long as I deem fit. And I deemed fit for long enough to dispatch the mother and have a play in the morgue.'

'You have only one option,' said Doctor Bohn, as if reading her mind. 'Make way. Run from your mind, and the boy will live. Let. Her. In.'

The child's hand pushed the knife, and blood leaked from his shoulder.

'Stop!' shouted Daphne. She didn't know what she was going to do. All she knew was she would stop them. Whatever that took. 'Stop!'

'Then run from your little mind, ant, and let her in.'

Daphne stopped herself from replying. The word *no* was well on the way to her lips, but she had stopped herself from speaking it. She could keep saying no, and Alfie would die, horribly and painfully. And yet her only other option was to say yes. To let the demon into her mind. To lose. To put the whole world at risk.

'Yes? Or no? Tell us, ant, we need to know whether to cut.'

Daphne sat in silence. Neither of those words were things she could say. And yet silence meant no. Silence meant death for Alfie.

'All great things come in threes,' said the demon in the doctor. 'Including great countdowns. And this one is going to be fun. Now, answer us.'

Daphne stared back at the doctor in silence.

'Three,' he said, staring back.

Daphne's mind felt blank.

'Two,' said the doctor with a smile.

A *yes* almost formed on Daphne's tongue. *Do not say yes,* said a soft voice from deep inside her mind. It had sounded like her mother.

'One,' said the doctor, and the child smiled and gripped the knife harder.

'Silence means go,' said Mrs Legge.

Dong.

When the doorbell chimed, the heads of the three possessed bodies whipped around. The child dropped the knife and jumped down from the stool. All three stood and hastened out of the room towards the kitchen. The doorbell chimed again as a loud clatter came through the hallway, followed by the sound of a lock turning. The demons were leaving through the back door.

Daphne approached the front door slowly, wondering if this was good news, some kind of saviour, or just another trick of the demons. She looked through the spyhole. Outside, looking straight back at her, was Agatha Hunter.

She mouthed, 'Hurry up and open,' and Daphne opened the door. She didn't want to. Agatha Hunter was possibly there to finish her off. But if she wasn't there, the demons would surely come back.

Mrs Hunter closed the door and towered over Daphne. She said, 'This is not a good place to start torture. The work seems half done already.' Then she stepped past Daphne, walked down the hallway into the kitchen, and closed the door.

Daphne leaned against the wall and caught her breath. A minute later, a familiar tone whistled from the kitchen stove and an annoyed woman groaned and tutted.

Chapter Eighteen

IN THE LOUNGE, THOUGH the possessed bodies were gone, the dinner table remained to taunt Daphne, piskie meat and all.

Seeing the tablecloth hang down like that was strangely nostalgic. Daphne had loved special occasions as a kid, when the long tablecloth would come out and give her a whole new secure hiding place under the table. And right now, with Sara's mother in the house, who was just as terrifying as she had been when Daphne was a child, she wanted to curl up, close her eyes, and wait for everything go away. She found herself on all fours, seeking comfort in the way that had worked as a small child. She crawled to the table, ducked her head beneath the cloth and slid under. There she collapsed to her side and squeezed her eyes shut, hoping everything would just go away.

When her hand came to its final resting position on the floor, she felt it again.

The knobble.

The bump under the carpet still felt so familiar, somehow friendly.

Footsteps grew louder from the kitchen, moving down the hallway. Daphne, a child again, peered out from her hiding place to see the open lounge door. Two huge boots stopped and turned towards her.

'Look at me,' said the deep voice of Mrs Hunter. 'Look at me!' the voice bellowed.

Daphne pushed the tablecloth up to see Mrs Hunter standing in the doorway holding a tray of tea, staring at her as daggers flew from her eyes. 'Hiding now? Pathetic. Do you wish to die hiding or fighting?'

Daphne stared back with no answer.

'*Surrendering* may be the appropriate word, I feel,' said Mrs Hunter, shaking her head. 'Worry not, Daphne. I will hang the coward that I am staring at right now. I will destroy her. But first, I have work to do.' Mrs Hunter turned and left. Daphne watched her feet thump up the stairs and again fell onto her side in her childhood hiding place; it really bloody hurt.

She had landed shoulder-first onto the hard knobble.

Daphne waited under the table for what felt like hours. Waiting for Agatha Hunter to leave, or to come back down and finish her. In a way, that was better than the demons doing it. If Mrs Hunter were to give her the death penalty for killing Sara, then at least the demons would not take her. And, for the world, that was the best possible thing. Mrs Hunter would know that.

Finally, footsteps appeared and got louder and lower, and the second step creaked. The footsteps kept going towards the front door. The door squeaked open, Daphne felt the cold air flood in, and the door thudded shut.

Daphne was alone. It felt that way, anyway, though that didn't stop her crawling out slowly, and peering around the doorway down the hall and into the kitchen. There was no one there. The demons seemed to have long gone. Looking the other way towards the front door, Daphne confirmed that Mrs Hunter had left too.

She stood, shaking, wrapping her arms around herself, taunted by the infernal whirr of the coin upstairs and the knowledge that she was far weaker than everything that waited outside.

If the demons turned up and threatened Alfie again, she would buckle and she knew it. She couldn't go through that again. The demons had a winning plan. The only way she wasn't going to give up and let the demons into her mind was if Mrs Hunter finished her off first. Neither sounded as appealing as grabbing that knife and going into the woods in a heroic fit of piskie stabby-stabby, or allowing herself the illusion of an escape to the golden beaches and a happy forever after. That idea was just a fantasy now. The world just wasn't going to let her.

Daphne had never felt so alone. She needed a friend. But she had no one to call on, or at least no one she would risk dragging into this whole thing.

Except, she did.

Olivia. The thought of her friend brought her hope. Hope felt good.

Daphne quickly found some energy. She opened her laptop, clicked through to her social media messages, and saw Olivia at the top. Her last message to her remained unread. Daphne typed another one anyway, requesting urgent help, and sent it.

She stared at her screen. At the message. At the tiny icon that would change colour the moment Olivia opened and read. Nothing changed. As she stared, a creaking sound came through the door.

It had come from her mother's bedroom.

Chapter Nineteen

DAPHNE STARED AT HER mother's closed door. The clicks started again, and stopped. Daphne approached slowly. Silently. She put her fingertips on the handle.

It felt cold. The wood looked old and dry. She had so many happy memories of bursting through this door. Whatever was about to happen, this would not become one of them.

The handle moved smoothly and easily and she slowly pushed open the door and tentatively peered around the corner with one eye.

Three mannequins were looking at her.

Plastic Deanna Tamblyn blinked.

The eyes on the other mannequins were plastic still, but some colour was beginning to form in them. The red hair was longer atop Morwenna Rowe's head. Gugwana's entire mouth was lifelike, the lips looked soft. They moved.

All three mannequin heads looked straight at her.

A tray of empty mugs sat on her mother's bed. Surely Mrs Hunter wasn't reanimating witches with cups of tea?

Daphne approached the mannequin in Sara's clothes. The figure was still as plastic as the moment she had dressed it. She felt sadness all over again when she realised that her mother's mannequin still looked as lifeless as ever. Still, she closed her eyes and hugged it. After being tortured by a demon inside Mrs Legge wearing her clothes, it felt like she was being ripped from her all over again. The mannequin was so hard and cold and lifeless. Whatever feeling she had hoped might come from the hug with the mannequin, nothing came at all. Nothing but disappointment and a fear creeping in. The fear that she was going to have to accept she was never going to see her again. It felt like a whole new level of pain and grief was coming for her.

As if she had long enough for that to happen.

When she stepped back from the mannequin and studied its hard, plastic face, she finally felt it, there and then. It was over. She wasn't coming back. And yet something was different. Something she could see from the corner of her eyes. She looked to her left. The mannequin in Gugwana's clothes was pointing up towards a tall cupboard. Daphne looked up at it, then at the mannequin. Then at Deanna Tamblyn's eyes, which blinked frantically, looking at her, then at the cupboard, then back at her.

Daphne turned and looked at the wooden cupboard door. She always respected her mother's privacy and had never looked in there before. When she looked back, two more arms were pointing at the cupboard, one on each mannequin.

Daphne pulled the stool from her mother's antique dressing table and climbed up, her tired and nervous knee wobbling, and pulled the door open.

The space was empty.

Plastic creaked. Morwenna Rowe's outstretched plastic finger bent and hooked downwards. It was moving. The mannequin was really moving. The old witches were really coming back. And they wanted her to find something.

Daphne pushed a hand into the cupboard well above her eye level, and felt along the dusty shelf. She looked around at the mannequins, and the bent plastic finger bobbed up and down.

Daphne tried again, pushing her hand in as far as it would go, fingertips feeling along the old chipboard. And then there it was. Something slid along as she touched it. It was thin and light. Dry. Paper. She slid it towards her and managed to slide a finger underneath. Gripping it between her thumb and finger, she pulled it out.

A notebook.

She looked back at the mannequins, all their arms down by their sides, a huge smile on Gugwana's face.

Daphne stepped down and opened a random page. It was full of her mother's handwriting. Pages and pages of it.

Bittersweet excitement rushed through her. It was like the first new contact she had had with her mother since the day she'd died.

The pad was full of all sorts. Poems. Recipes. Notes. Diary entries.

She stopped on a page with a poem and sat on the bed, her heart in her mouth, and read.

Oh, for Daphne
In the middle of the vastest ocean,
A thousand miles from home,
A bottle cork floated by.
No one saw it;
No one knew;
It floated by alone.

A thousand miles from the nearest evil,
Floating on the sea,
The bottle cork safely sailed.
The beast was silent;
As it came from below;
And dragged it down alone.

At the bottom of the deepest ocean,
A wet old world from home,
A bottle cork fractured and died.
No one saw it;
No one knew;
It fell apart alone.

Daphne turned the page. The next line shocked her.

Dear Daphne, this poem is for you. I'm still working on your epilogue, when I find the time.

She turned the page, excited to see the final verses of her poem. It was just full of a whole load of scrawled notes. Nonsensical. She turned another page.

It was a list.

A list of the herbs in the old ornate rack.

Love salt. Use 6-10 grains for the experience of love. Six to ten? Daphne must have given Olivia a few hundred.

Devil's Fungus. For inducing hallucinations and dire experiences of terror. Warning; a dose of more than one piece will lead to an irreversible nightmare which generally ends in suicide. Use in case of emergency only. Antidote: 6-7 grains of love salt and a kick up the backside administered immediately after.

Now she knew why the lid had been on so tight.

Coletta Floretta. Placebo; 100% Pure Belief; it's just sliced and dried carrot.

Daphne laughed a little at that, especially as she again noticed her mother's constant use of semicolons, almost always in the wrong place. It was one of those little things, her personality sitting there on the pages.

Daphne's eyes were taken by movement and the smile rushed from her face. Movement from the mannequins. They were all pointing again, one towards the door, two down at the floor in the direction of the kitchen. Deanna Tamblyn's eyes blinked furiously.

And then a cackle came from downstairs. Inside.

A piskie.

The laughs erupted as small footsteps pattered across the carpet, and pots and pans clattered in the kitchen. The piskies had got into the house.

Chapter Twenty

Daphne looked up at the three mannequins, desperate for some kind of guidance. They delivered. All three were now pointing back at her own bedroom. She rushed out of the room and closed the door behind her. Glancing around the corner down the stairs, she saw the back of a green-dressed piskie opening the front door. She watched as more piskies piled in. Swarms of them.

The back door. The demons had left that way and she hadn't locked it. How stupid.

They saw her. And they laughed.

The first piskie raced for the stairs, then another, then another, and Daphne darted backwards and into her own room, slamming the door shut and twisting the lock quickly. She pushed her shoulder against the door and waited. Sure enough, seconds later, she felt banging on the other side, followed by chittering voices and cackling laughter. The bangs weren't hard. The creatures were small, and to get in, they'd surely need some kind of tool. She'd be safe in there. Unless they were joined by the demons. The demons would smash through with no problems at all.

Daphne braced herself against the door, although the banging was slowing. She could still hear some outside too, a tiny-voiced crowd all over the house, inside and out. Scrapes and bangs came up the stairs and through the floorboards. Stupid laughter punctuated the crowd noise. And then, as quickly as it had begun, it faded away. A minute later, the whole house fell deathly quiet. There wasn't a single sound.

Nothing at all.

Nothing but the sound of Daphne breathing.

Nothing but the old pipes groaning.

Nothing but a golden coin on her desk, spinning and whirring.

Were the piskies really gone? Or were they tricking her? She pressed her ear up against the wood and listened. She held her breath. There wasn't so much as a creak.

Daphne pulled herself away from the door and looked around her room for a weapon. There wasn't anything. How could she be so stupid? Of course she needed a weapon to hand. But she had nothing to fight with. Nothing but her fists. Sure, the piskies were about three feet tall, but there were hundreds of them. Hundreds, or, hopefully, now none, although that didn't really make any sense.

Daphne slowly turned the handle and poised herself ready to slam the door shut again and brace herself against the old wood. She pulled the door gently open, just a slight slit, and peered through with one eye. There was no movement, no noise. She pulled the door open wider and looked around the corner. All was quiet. All so still.

Daphne stepped across the hallway and gently opened her mother's bedroom door. And gasped silently.

The mannequins still held out their arms, outstretched pointing as they had been. Except for the one with the live eyes. Gripped in the smooth hand of the outstretched plastic arm of Deanna Tamblyn hung a lifeless piskie. It swayed ever so slightly, the plastic fingers wrapped tightly around its neck. Daphne stared at the small face. The creature looked so old, so harmless now it was dead. The mannequin started to tip under the weight of the piskie's body, then fell to the floor, the plastic bouncing rigidly on the carpet, the dead piskie crumpled in a heap. As Daphne stared at the floor, a horrible feeling overcame her. Something was missing. Her mother's scrapbook was no longer on the floor. It was gone. Anger flared up inside her. Anger mixed with loss, and finally, with acceptance.

She walked to her mother's mannequin with tears in her eyes, and stared at its shiny plastic face. Her mother was never coming back. Her small tears turned to small sobs, and she turned around, unable to look at the generic plastic face anymore. On the floor beneath her, the piskie's body slumped further. The mannequin had released its grasp. Daphne picked up Deanna Tamblyn's mannequin from its prone position, placed it back on its feet, looked at its eyes, so full of life, and turned to leave the room. She still had a house to check for live piskies.

She turned and walked to the top of the stairs, anger in her gut and a renewed sense of loss for her mother. She looked down the stairs. No piskies. But something was wrong. The old coat rack was gone, Daphne's coats and umbrella with it. As Daphne walked down, stepping over the creaky step, she noticed that the old bristled doormat had gone too.

She turned at the bottom and walked down the bare hallway. She didn't need to open the lounge door. It wasn't there. Not even the hinges. She looked into the lounge and saw nothing. The piskies had taken everything. Aside from the carpet and some shards of broken mirror, there was nothing left.

Nothing at all.

Daphne raced to the kitchen. The old knife rack was gone. A space where the table was. The old ornate spice rack: gone. The old whistling kettle and huge old iron pots: all gone. The place was completely empty. The piskies had utterly cleaned out the house on Hanging Hill Lane. The single thing that they hadn't taken was a tatty paperback copy of M.L. Rayner's book *Echoes of Home*, a book that Daphne hadn't enjoyed and now not even the piskies wanted either.

The bathroom revealed the same emptiness. The shower curtain: gone. Toothbrush and toiletries: gone. The cupboard from the wall: gone. Even the toilet seat and cistern lid. It was all gone.

There was nothing left.

Nothing but the old wooden backing to a broken mirror, which had been moved from the lounge to the kitchen and discarded on the floor.

Gone: all the textbooks left to her by her mother. Gone: the lounge table, chairs, sofas, the television, the paintings that had hung on the wall, including one that Daphne had painted. Gone: the photo album of Daphne and her mother. Gone: Alfie's box of toys, some of which had been hers too when she was a child.

And then it hit her. Gone: the old box of her childhood toys.

All gone. Daphne's childhood was gone.

Every last connection to her childhood from her toys to her mother, everything, aside from this old house on Hanging Hill Lane and the memories inside her head: gone.

But the thing that hurt the most wasn't any of those things. Not even the ornate spice rack or the witches' spices it contained. No sooner than she had found it, the piskies had taken her mother's notebook. Her last chance for connection. Her whole past had gone, and with it, the last chance of reconnecting with a part of her mother that she had never had the chance to while she was alive.

Those piskies. Those piskies would pay.

As Daphne stood alone in the middle of the room alone and aghast, she noticed one thing the piskies hadn't taken, aside from the carpet. The thing that was *underneath* the carpet.

The knobble.

The last connection between Daphne and her younger self. The one thing the piskies hadn't taken was the one thing they couldn't find.

Daphne walked over to the knobble and rested her foot on it. The bump still felt so familiar, even without the old table above it.

'What are you?' she said gently, and then looked to the corner of the floor. She walked over, dropped to her knees, and tugged. The carpet was stiff and didn't want to budge, and Daphne found herself first frustrated, and then angered. And then, slowly at first, up it came, peeling up in her hand, leaving Daphne coughing in a cloud of dust.

She gripped the corner of the carpet and walked back towards and then past the knobble, revealing the old floorboards under the carpet. And there it was. The real thing behind the knobble. A handle, a catch, and a padlock. To a cellar. Daphne's house had a cellar.

And suddenly everything made sense. Sara's house next door had a cellar, in that exact same place. A cellar that didn't seem to have a bottom. Daphne didn't remember Sara's having a padlock.

Something down there needed to be locked away.

Something moved behind Daphne, catching her attention and spinning her around as her heart jumped into her throat.

Daphne dropped the carpet, which rolled back into place.

Agatha Hunter stood in the doorway, staring at her. Finally, she spoke. 'You let them take everything. Go to your room, Daphne. I will follow you up when I am ready.' Mrs

Hunter produced a metal hook from behind her, looked at the spiked end then back at Daphne. 'You have failed. Your world is about to end, and I am here to facilitate that forthwith. Go, now.' Agatha Hunter glared as Daphne stared back, frozen to the spot, and screamed, 'Go!' The sound rattled around the empty house, shaking the curtainless windows and doorless frames.

So Daphne went.

She had nothing else left to give or lose.

Nothing at all.

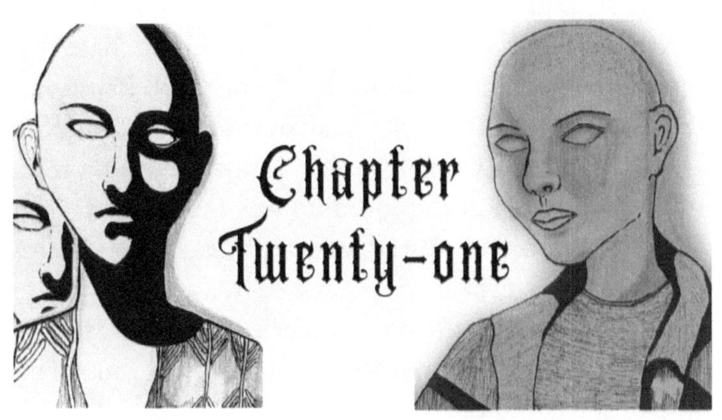

Chapter Twenty-one

'ABOUT MY DAUGHTER. My grandchild.'

Daphne was shaking as she stood in her room feeling like a small child. And yet she couldn't blame Mrs Hunter. She was right. Daphne had caused the death of her daughter.

Agatha Hunter stepped forward. Daphne stepped back away from her, scared of what she might do if she made contact. Not that a witch like Agatha Hunter needed physical contact to destroy someone if she wanted to. She could probably do it with a wink of an eye.

'Daphne Locke. I cannot promise this will be painless. I cannot promise I will not enjoy it. I can promise that when it is over, I will do what I can to undo your work with my family. Until then, lie down.'

Daphne stared back, utter dread in her stomach, and stepped back further, feeling her mattress at the back of her knees.

'Daphne Locke.' Agatha Hunter glowered at Daphne, and Daphne knew it was all over. Agatha raised her hand. Daphne didn't even feel the force that pushed her back and bound her to her bed. It was like the demon pinning her down all over again, except now, it was all just magic. She couldn't move anything from her neck down. All she could do was burst into tears.

Agatha Hunter stared at Daphne. 'You kill my daughter. My grandson is possessed by a demon, at your fault. And you are the one who cries like a coward?'

Daphne's cries turned to panicked sobs. 'I'm sorry,' was all she could blub.

'Sorry?' bellowed Agatha Hunter. 'Sorry? Were you sorry when you swapped the clothes with a piskie? To selfishly save yourself? Sorry? My grandson died after eating fishhooks. I cannot imagine suffering something so painful.'

Agatha Hunter raised her arms at her sides, floated a foot above the ground, and flew towards Daphne on the bed, her face contorted with rage.

'You were not ready. I knew you were not ready. I made that so, so clear. So now, here we are. At your final confession.'

Daphne heard the words but her foggy mind took a moment to register what they meant. 'My what?' said Daphne through her tears.

'Your confession, my dear. And, just like the confessions of old, pain will be deeply involved. There is nothing I can do about that. Now, wait there.' Mrs Hunter almost laughed as she left the room, leaving Daphne pinned down, panicking, breathing so fast that her head was feeling light.

The more she struggled against the invisible forces, the tighter they squeezed and the lighter her head got. She had no choice but to stop the struggle. Stop the fight. Give up.

Mrs Hunter returned and before Daphne knew what had happened, she found herself blind, her eyes bound firmly shut and however hard she tried, they would not open. The last thing she had seen was the quickest glimpse of Mrs Hunter entering holding what appeared to be a length of rope.

'Have a look around, see what you can find,' said the voice of Mrs Hunter.

Daphne stared into the darkness of her mind. It seemed like a lonely place. And then the screwing sound started from the other side of the room, up high, like something twisting and creaking into the ceiling. It was barely louder than the whirr of the spinning coin, and all sounded loud and clear in the otherwise quiet room with her vision removed and her sense of hearing intensifying.

'Have you ever seen a noose be tied?' asked Mrs Hunter as Daphne's eyelids were released. Mrs Hunter stood over her. She looped the rope around itself, and with a pull and a twist, a perfectly formed noose dangled from her hand.

'Now,' she said, placing the noose over the back of the desk chair. Daphne watched on in terror as Mrs Hunter floated up to the ceiling, and tugged at a metal object that protruded from the ceiling beam seeming to test its strength. When she let go, it was clear what it was. The hook.

'Is the picture becoming clear yet, my dear?' asked Mrs Hunter. 'Did you ever even stop to wonder from where this street got its name?' Mrs Hunter retrieved the rope and tied the straight end around the hook. When she let go, a noose dangled a foot under the beam. Below that, plenty of room for Daphne to dangle and die.

Mrs Hunter returned to the bedside. 'Last chance. Confess.'

'I did it. I'm not denying anything. I'm so sorry. I was fooled. I was so stupid.'

'No!' bellowed back Agatha Hunter. 'Every time you do not confess, I will turn the mind-screws tighter. Tighter and tighter until it feels like your brain will burst and slop through your ears and squeeze through your eyes. Now, confess!'

'I'm guilty!' shouted Daphne in desperation.

'That you are. Watch my fingers, Daphne Locke.' Agatha Hunter raised one hand and gently rubbed the tips of her thumb and forefinger together in a small soft circle. And with each rotation, Daphne felt rising pain shoot through her mind and the forces around her constrict.

'Stop it, I'm sorry, please!' shouted Daphne.

Agatha Hunter's fingers stopped, and the pain subsided. 'Confess. What are you, Daphne Locke? I need accuracy. You will need to be specific for the pain to stop.'

Daphne thought and thought. She hadn't denied anything. She was guilty. And her confession wasn't enough. 'I don't know what you want to hear,' she sobbed. The fingers moved again, and Daphne's brain felt like it was going to pop out of her skull. 'Stop, please!'

'Confess and I shall stop. What are you?'

'I'm stupid. A stupid bad witch. A useless witch. Just stupid,' she cried, and looked at Agatha Hunter to see if her fingers would move again. They did, and the pain reached new levels as Daphne was sure she felt the pressure push some liquid out from one ear.

'Confess, child, your brain is starting to come out,' Agatha Hunter said calmly, and Daphne felt herself give up hope and let go of any chance of life.

'I'm broken. I'm a broken witch.'

The fingers moved again and Daphne's whole body twisted and contorted with the pain.

'You are not being honest! I need honesty before I release you from this world.'

And there it was, as if she needed it. Mrs Hunter had said it. Daphne's final confirmation that after this pain was over, she was to be killed. Executed. Put down by her best friend's mother, a woman she had feared since the day she took her first step. That fear, it turned out, was warranted. Like the witches of old, she was to be hanged.

'What are you, Daphne?'

Daphne's head hurt too much to think. She had confessed to everything she thought Agatha Hunter wanted to hear.

'I'm a bad friend,' she said quietly. She looked at Agatha's fingers. They didn't move.

'I'll give you that one for it is true. But that is not what I am waiting to hear, and I am growing impatient. I have so much more pain in these fingertips. You have not yet experienced true pain, Daphne Locke, and if you do not confess, I will not release you before you experience it. Do you understand?'

Daphne didn't understand. She had no idea what she was being asked.

'Confess!' came a bellowing voice that made the walls shake. 'Confess and I shall release you from this pain.'

'I confess!' shouted Daphne, not knowing where the impulse to shout was coming from. She just felt numb now. Emotionally ruined by days of torture from the demons, sleep deprivation, slaps and smacks from children with sticks, assaults by piskies and, more than the rest, the realisation she would never be able to save her mother. And the guilt. Such guilt. 'I confess,' she said quietly, almost past caring if more pain would come or not.

'To what?'

'To not caring if you are going to hurt me again.'

Mrs Hunter stepped forward towards the bed, and stopped. 'Better.' She scratched her nose. 'But that is not what I am looking for. Now tell me. What. Are. You?'

'I'm a shit witch,' she said.

'No!' boomed Agatha Hunter, rubbing her finger and thumb and sending Daphne writhing in pain. 'We are going backwards now. Go forward into your confession, and then I will release you. Tell me, now!'

Daphne lay on her childhood bed, unable to move, helpless and exhausted, and looked out of the window, desperate to see stars shine where the moon used to be, a sign that her mother was there, her last chance for some source of strength. But the full moon shone bright.

Agatha Hunter pointed at the moon, raised her finger, and the moon shone brighter. 'She is not here to save you. Now, what are you?'

'I'm...'

'Go on...'

'I'm...'

'Quickly, my dear, you're dallying.'

'I'm...' Daphne didn't know what she was. A bad witch, an accidental child-killer, stupid, miserable, lonely, anxious, tired and more. And yet nothing felt like it would make any difference at all to Agatha Hunter, who would just inject her mind with pure pain whatever she said. So she said what she wanted to say instead. 'I'm... tired of dealing with this, with the demons, with you, I'm tired and I'm scared.'

'Some honesty at last. And that makes you, what?'

'I'm a coward!' blurted out Daphne, with the feeling that she had finally said something with enough honesty that Mrs Hunter might accept it and put her out of her misery.

'What makes you so? Do tell me before I get annoyed with you.'

'I did it. I swapped the clothes because I was a coward. I didn't want to die. I knew deep down that I was swapping with someone. I panicked, I swapped, because I am a useless stupid coward.' Daphne burst into more tears. 'There. I've told you now.'

'Nice try,' said Agatha Hunter as she raised her fingers and the pain in Daphne's mind and body shot to new heights.

'I'm so tired of this,' mumbled Daphne in a beaten whisper, allowing it to comfort her, feeling the end coming and the peace that it might finally bring.

'We're all tired, my dear girl. And I am running out of time and patience.'

Tell her, whispered a voice from deep within Daphne's mind.

'I don't know what I'm supposed to say,' Daphne whispered back at both Agatha Hunter and the voice that had come from within.

Agatha Hunter leaned over Daphne. 'My dear girl, you know exactly what you are.'

Say it, whispered the voice inside. *Tell her, and set us free.*

Daphne was exhausted. She'd been dealing with all of this for far too long now. So fuck Agatha Hunter. Fuck her. Daphne was only twenty years old, only a couple of feet taller than a piskie, living alone, grieving, single-handedly fighting real demons, piskies, and god only knew what else. She wasn't perfect, but she was doing a damned good job. Or at least she was before that one mistake. And even now, she was fighting, still guarding the old house, not running away. Keeping the agreement she had made with her mother. And actually, that made her pretty damn brave. There was always that spark of strength somewhere deep inside her, however bad the pain of life got, and that made her brave. *So, fuck you, Mrs Hunter.*

Say that, whispered the voice from within. *No*, replied a firm thought.

'You know what you are!' shouted Agatha Hunter.

You know, whispered the voice. *Say it. Tell her.*

'I'm brave!' Daphne shouted with all the conviction of someone who knew their words to be true.

Even if it would evoke the wrath of the woman who was about to kill her, at least she would go out finally admitting to herself that she was not scared like she had always believed herself to be, but brave. Incredibly so. The parting shot to go out on her terms felt good, some fitting confirmation that it was true.

Now tell her to fuck herself, whispered the distant voice. *I'm not* that *brave*, Daphne thought back to herself.

'I'm brave.'

Mrs Hunter dropped her hand to her side, and her lines relaxed and a smile spread across her face. 'And there, finally, we have your confession.' She took a long breath and took one of Daphne's hands in both of hers. 'And now, you are released.'

Daphne felt the constricting stop, her lungs free up, and freedom return to her body. The pain left her head.

'I thought that was going to take you forever. And now, finally, you are ready, sister.'

Daphne stared back at Agatha Hunter. She looked completely different. Soft, likeable, shining.

'Are you going to kill me?' It didn't look like it.

'Don't be daft, dear. There are three demons out there, my grandson is occupied by one of them and I am waylaid in bringing back my daughter. I need you. But I needed you to be ready. You did not believe and you were hiding in textbooks instead of getting ready. You had not yet confessed to yourself. And now you have.'

'Confessed what?'

'Oh, my dear. Do not make me repeat. We have dallied enough.'

'That I am brave?'

'Indeed. Although I would have preferred if you *had* told me to fuck myself, but we got close enough. Anyway, we must work fast to make up the time. Wait there, and do not move.'

Agatha Hunter left the bedroom, leaving Daphne on the bed, confused, but able to catch her breath. Something felt different. As Agatha had dropped her hand that last time and taken all the pain from her head, it felt like something else had gone with it. She couldn't quite picture what it was that had left her, or if it was a feeling in her body or in her mind. Something was missing, and as a result, she felt good. Lighter. Strong.

Footsteps thudded from the other side of the door, as though Agatha Hunter was wrestling something heavy up the stairs. The door flew open, and a human stumbled in, a cloth bag over his head. He tripped and fell hard on the floor as he struggled viciously, his hands tied tight behind him. Daphne recognised the smart suit immediately. It had a timepiece hanging from the breast pocket. Mrs Hunter removed the cloth bag, revealing the face of Doctor Bohn, eyes glowing red and jaws snapping at her face.

'Right,' said Agatha Hunter, 'help me get him up there.'

'Where?'

Mrs Hunter looked up at the rope hanging from the ceiling. 'The noose.'

Daphne's jaw dropped. To dispatch the demon, Agatha Hunter was going to hang Doctor Bohn.

Chapter Twenty-two

Daphne's mind fell blank and her body went stiff. Doctor Bohn had been a lovely man who had helped her through a time of need. And now Agatha Hunter was going to hang him to kill the demon inside.

'Help me, dear,' said Mrs Hunter, and the desk chair seemed to roll over to her all by itself.

'What about Doctor Bohn? We can draw the demon out first, use a siren.' She couldn't let this happen. Nor could she stop Agatha Hunter from doing whatever she would do, however brave she now believed she was.

'Inconsequential,' said Mrs Hunter, 'and we do not play with the sirens. Okay, I'll do it myself.' She wrestled the fighting figure of Doctor Bohn from the floor, his teeth gnashing at her, his bound feet kicking back, eyes glowing red. 'Right, watch.' She leaned back, followed by an almighty headbutt smack in the back of the doctor's head.

He seemed stunned for a second, and Mrs Hunter gripped him hard as the pair floated up together. Daphne watched helplessly at Doctor Bohn's head being pushed through the noose, his body lowered down and the rope pulled tight around his neck as Mrs Hunter floated back down to the ground.

'Now,' said Mrs Hunter. All good things come in threes, and that includes lessons. So let's move on to part two. Beyond the three, the rest will remain for you to work out.'

Dread filled Daphne's stomach. She hadn't had even a minute to recover from her last lesson, and that had shaken her to her core, a brutal assault on her psyche just to make a point. And yet, deep down, she knew it. Without that pain, without that force of nature and that brutal lesson, she would never have accepted it. But she wasn't yet ready for another lesson. She just couldn't cope with another psychological beating like that. But Mrs Hunter wasn't saying anything.

Doctor Bohn had been a kind man, another victim of the demons, and deserved to be hanged as little as all the innocent women of the past.

'Oh take that worried look off your face, it doesn't suit you anymore,' said Mrs Hunter. 'He's not going to die. This is a lesson in rescue, not killing. No-nonsense, godless exorcism, if you like. Now, do what you do, and be brave.'

Daphne watched, confused, hoping that Mrs Hunter wasn't actually going to harm him.

Mrs Hunter looked at her as she gripped Doctor Bohn's possessed body hard from behind in a tight bear hug.

'He's going to be okay, right? That's Doctor Bohn, my therapist,' said Daphne, heart full of worry.

'Of course he is. I'm not evil. Right, let's free the poor man.'

'What do you mean by *free*?'

'Now,' said Mrs Hunter as she stepped towards Daphne, Doctor Bohn's body hanging, flapping in the noose behind her. 'The sisters, when they came two years ago, also gave you three lessons, did they not? Repeat them to me.'

'Three lessons?' Daphne asked, with absolutely no idea what she was talking about.

'I assume they turned up and put on some theatrics for you. That wasn't just for show, my dear. Spoon-feeding doesn't teach. Working out from clues, using your head, that teaches, that is how we learn. Now, what were the three lessons?'

Doctor Bohn kicked and flailed behind her as he hung by his neck.

Daphne thought back to the time the three old witches had saved her the first time the demons had come. And there was a lesson that she remembered well. It had saved her the first time she was alone with a demon. 'Sometimes,' she said quietly, 'to be seen, you need a bit of colour.'

'Right. One! What was lesson two?'

Daphne didn't know, and her thoughts were distracted by Doctor Bohn's possessed head trying and failing to grab the rope above with his teeth.

'Stop looking at him, he will be just fine. What was lesson two?'

'Spells must end in a rhyme?'

'No!' Mrs Hunter's voice boomed. 'You must by now know that not to be true. So it cannot have been the lesson. So what was the lesson behind that? The lesson behind the pretence?'

Daphne stuttered.

'Did it work? The rhymes?' asked Mrs Hunter.

'Yes.'

'But that's not how magic works and you know it.'

'I know. Now. But only because I studied the books.'

'So how did it work for you? It worked well enough to dispatch that demon, did it not?'

'Yes.'

'And yet that is not how it works. So, how?'

Daphne thought, the fog of tiredness and fear slowing her brain. Mrs Hunter was right. She had used a fake method to great effect. A word found its way to her mouth. 'Placebo?'

'Close!' called Mrs Hunter. 'Warm. Now go for hot.'

'Because I believed it?'

'Yes! Finally, we have arrived!'

'It worked because I believed it?' Daphne was so confused, trying to work out what exactly Mrs Hunter meant.

'That was lesson two, and you have done well enough, so I will spell it out for you, if you will excuse the pun. If you believe hard enough, my dear, reality will bend to your way and your will. And if you apply that belief to yourself, well, let's just say that's where the magic happens.'

Daphne was shocked. They'd planned it all along. Self-belief and belief in the magic. That was the combination. It was no wonder two years of burying her head in the textbooks hadn't worked. She'd never believed she was worthy.

'Be brave enough to believe, and believe enough to be brave, Daphne.'

Daphne nodded. Doctor Bohn yanked left and right and thrashed about on the rope, face contorting.

'Lesson three,' said Mrs Hunter with a sly grin growing from nowhere.

Daphne stood still, looking back, concern about Doctor Bohn returning to her as he kicked his tied legs hard in all directions, a fish on a line. 'Are you sure he's okay?'

'The man will be fine. The demon, however, is fucked. Now, lesson three.'

'I don't know.' Daphne had no idea.

'Oh come on my dear, they will have drilled this one home, you couldn't have helped but notice.'

'I didn't.'

'Well obviously, you're doing the thing now that they made it very clear not to do.'

Daphne had no idea. She went to speak, then stopped herself.

'There.' Mrs Hunter jabbed Daphne in the stomach with an outstretched finger. 'You did it again.'

'Did what?' There was a long pause as they stared at each other, the demon hanging from the ceiling now trying to yank the hook down by bouncing up and down by his neck.

'You're doing it right now, and they will have said not to do it time after time after time.'

'What?'

'You're taking a long time to get there, my dear. Doing as they said not to do. Over and over and over again, one would hope, for the lesson to be learned, though you are doing what they said not to do in learning the very lesson of what it is you were supposed to learn.'

Something almost came to Daphne. 'Don't...' She stopped again.

'And again, dear, you're doing it again.'

'Dally! They said don't dally!'

'Yes!' said Mrs Hunter. 'Do not dilly dally. Hesitation is the window through which self-doubt creeps in. Hesitation is what kills the belief. Hesitation harms bravery.' Mrs Hunter looked over her shoulder at Doctor Bohn's demon, now swinging slowly, glowering at her with red eyes, tongue hanging out loosely. Then she shot a look at Daphne and spoke quickly. 'Hesitation kills self-belief. Killing the belief will kill the magic. And that is what might kill this man. And so we will not dally, lest we accidentally kill the man. Now, turn your eyes this way, watch, witch.'

Mrs Hunter turned around, grabbed Doctor Bohn's tied torso by the waist and, in a flash, yanked it down hard.

Daphne's eyes widened and jaw dropped as her hands landed over her mouth, but the savage crack of the doctor's neck never came, and though Daphne expected to now see the dead doctor swing, instead, her therapist's body fell clean away, landing on the floor in front of her, breathing heavily, if not conscious. When she looked up, the rope still stretched taut.

Hanging in the rope, in its real and true form, horned head above the tight noose and scaley body underneath, was a demon.

The beast stank of death.

Chapter Twenty-three

THE DEMON STARED AT Daphne through red eyes with fire burning inside them. A forked tongue lashed out of a sharp-toothed mouth towards her, jutting out almost three feet before stopping just short of her face. But the rope and the hook held firm, and anger spread across the scaley face of the demon. It twisted its head hard and fast, whacking its sharp horn into the rope.

'Is it secure?' asked Daphne, watching the rope hold its shape.

'As much as I believe it to be.'

Daphne took a moment to register the meaning. It was hard to think with a real demon hanging in your bedroom staring with evil in its eyes.

Doctor Bohn groaned on the floor, and Daphne dropped to her knees by his side. He opened his eyes and jumped, sending Daphne jumping too. He looked back at her, then up at the demon, went white as a sheet, and fainted.

'Is he going to be okay?' Daphne looked up at Mrs Hunter.

'As much as you believe he will be. I should not need to repeat these responses. Repetition is a terrible way to learn.'

This was not helping. What was it with these old witches and talking in riddles and lessons? She didn't want a lesson. She wanted the demon gone. Mrs Hunter just stared back at the beast, who had finally given up its struggle.

'You have read the memory magic, have you not?'

'Two years ago, maybe. I haven't used it.'

'I know.' Mrs Hunter looked down at Doctor Bohn and lightly prodded him in the gut with the toe of her shoe. 'Use it now.'

Daphne looked down at Doctor Bohn then back up at Mrs Hunter. 'Now?'

'Too late,' said Mrs Hunter. 'Do not dally. You have hesitated and your chance of untainted self-belief departed through the window which you left open.'

Daphne squeezed her eyes shut. She had failed to learn a lesson she had literally just been taught.

'Hesitation takes the magic from life, and the life from magic,' Mrs Hunter continued. 'Belief puts it in. The two are not compatible. You know the magic, you have studied it, do you remember it?

'Yes. I think.'

'Remember where the magic happens. Clear? Good. Now, use it, go. It will not harm him if you do not open the dilly-dallying window. Go.'

Daphne immediately dropped down alongside Doctor Bohn and covered his eyes with one hand. She then spread her fingers of that hand, reached through with the forefinger and thumb of the other, and opened his eye. Behind her, she heard Mrs Hunter turn and step away.

As Daphne made eye contact with the single open eye of Doctor Bohn, pictures flashed up in his eyeball. Pictures of him in his office falling asleep, and waking up with glowing red eyes. Pictures of him stalking the streets as a possessed man, and pictures of him sitting in Daphne's bathroom as she showered. Pictures of him eating dinner at her table. Pictures of him being captured by Mrs Hunter. Pictures of him hanging from a rope in Daphne's bedroom. Each picture flashed up and slid out from his eyeball onto the floor like his eye was printing tiny photographs, and one by one, they disappeared in a tiny green flame and puff of smoke which dissipated into the room around them. And then they were gone. When Daphne had finished, she released his eyelid and face, revealing an expression that was so familiar to her: the expression on the faces of the ladies on the beach, and on Penelope Pengilly the last time she had seen her. When she looked up, Mrs Hunter was gazing down at her.

'Good. Now, onto your next lesson.'

Another lesson. Daphne was done with lessons, but couldn't deny that she was suddenly feeling powerful. Special. Brave. The tiredness had left her body. She had the feeling that everything was somehow right. And considering there was a huge demon hanging in her bedroom, it was a feeling she was not expecting to feel. 'That was my first real magic,' she said, almost with a smile.

'Poppycock,' blurted Mrs Hunter, gesturing with her eyes at the coin that was still perpetually spinning on her desk. 'You do it without even trying. Why does it still spin? Curious, what goes on deep inside that mind of yours. Anyway, enough.' Mrs Hunter paused and sniffed, looking thoughtfully at the coin. 'The piskies would kill violently for a gold coin like that. They would rip you apart to get it. Release him.'

'Doctor Bohn?'

'Put him out the front door, my dear, he will stumble around like a drunken slug till someone picks him up and in three days will be right as a snail in the rain.'

Daphne looked back, all the things that were happening still processing.

'What have we learned about hesitation? Go, now.'

Daphne led the doctor slowly and carefully down the stairs, opened the front door, and led him down the path to the pavement. They stood there together, one a shell of a man, one a newly validated witch, neither knowing what to do. Eventually, Daphne simply took the shell of Doctor Bohn by the shoulders, turned him to face up the hill away from the dangers that lurked in the woods, and gave him the slightest nudge forward. He flinched at the touch, but then began to make his way up the hill, each step a whole-body jerk followed by a soft sway. Poor Doctor Bohn, he didn't deserve this. But it wasn't her fault. 'Sorry,

Doctor Bohn,' she whispered. 'You're so good to me.' But then, realising she was dallying, she tore her gaze away from the doctor, and hurried back inside. Mrs Hunter had been working her magic in Daphne's bedroom, and a tabletop Daphne had never seen before floated in the centre of the room. On top lay several items.

An ornate metal cigarette lighter engraved in an unknown script. A three-foot-long dead straight wrought-iron bar, spiked at each end. A curved blade the size of a forearm, shining in silver. A strange tool which looked like a giant pair of rusty nail clippers. That was the one that made her shudder, though her eyes were drawn back to the spiked iron.

'Now,' said Mrs Hunter. A lesson in dealing with the demon. In this session, one feels like one can be a little more direct. First, punishment with fire.'

Daphne noticed the slight wince on the demon's face.

'Now,' said Mrs Hunter. 'Do this.' She clicked her fingers and a flame shot up from the top of her thumb.

'How?' replied Daphne.

'Always waiting, hesitating, so there is no magic,' said Mrs Hunter, frustrated. She picked up the cigarette lighter and passed it to Daphne. 'Consider this your training wheels. Spark it.'

Daphne flicked open the lighter, which made a satisfying *chink*. She struck the wheel with her thumb and a flame danced on the wick. The demon winced and jerked his body as if trying to back away.

'Place the lighter under the chin,' said Mrs Hunter with a smile. The demon struggled and kicked. When Daphne reached up and the flame licked the demon's chin, the beast screeched with a volume and horrific intensity that had Daphne reeling back, her ears ringing. On its face, Daphne saw absolute agony. Water poured from its eyes. It was actually crying.

'But...' said Daphne, wanting to ask a question but wondering if it would be met with derision or just something else that wasn't a straight answer. 'But if demons live in Hell, why wouldn't they like fire? They are from Hell, right?'

'Yes,' said Mrs Hunter. 'Or a place enough like it. But if they liked it there, why would they not stay there? You are from your mother's womb, and you came out screaming and crying. Would you like to go back there? Or if we put you in a giant womb now would you not suffocate and die?'

That kind of made sense. Enough not to argue.

'And anyway, Hellfire is not the same. So, yes, fire. Fire created by the sisters is not a fire that agrees with them.' Mrs Hunter flicked up a small flame on her thumb again, pointed it towards the demon, and blew. Her breath ignited as it passed the flame and engulfed the demon, which screamed and screeched and yelled in agony so loudly that Daphne could see the glass in her windows shake. 'Feels good, doesn't it, my dear?'

'What?'

Mrs Hunter looked at the spinning coin again. 'Indecision and delaying. Hmm.'

Daphne felt for some reason that she might be in trouble. But there was no sense of judgement.

'Now,' said Mrs Hunter, 'grab the metal bar and add some fire to one end. Show me who you are.'

Daphne grabbed the bar and flicked the lighter.

'Cheater,' said Mrs Hunter with a hint of mischief in her grin. 'Thumbs, my dear, fingers and thumbs.'

Daphne smiled coyly as she heated one spiked end of the metal bar with the metal lighter. She followed an urge to blow gently on it and the flame roared a little higher, and the spike glowed like a medieval red-hot poker. She grinned at the smouldering end and basked in the scorching heat that radiated onto her face.

'Good fire ant!' said Mrs Hunter with a smile. 'Now, stick the glowing end two feet up his arsehole.'

Daphne was stunned, and her head shot around to see Mrs Hunter laughing, a sight she had never seen before.

'Joking, my dear. Unless you really want to. The arsehole is always an option, especially if you need a giggle. No, go for the eye.'

The demon wrestled against the rope as Daphne approached. She felt hesitant. 'Sure?'

'Did they torture you? Did they kill your neighbours? Did they kill your wonderful mother?'

Daphne felt a fire burn inside her.

'Did they kill my daughter? Our sisters?'

An inferno raged in Daphne's torso, and as it rose, the orange glow of the heated metal burned brighter.

'Did they take my grandson? My little Alfie? Then why dally, fire ant?'

Daphne was mad. She plunged the red-hot spike into the beast's eye, and the demon wailed and flailed and struggled and kicked as the hot poker hissed, and steam billowed from its eye socket into her bedroom. A few seconds later, the demon and the steam disappeared into nothingness.

The glowing metal faded to black, and Daphne's breathing faded to a steady pace.

Daphne looked at Mrs Hunter with a smile, feeling powerful. With an ally like this, she *was* powerful. She could get the revenge she was craving, and destroy all the demons. Together, they could save Alfie.

The empty space where the demon had been gave Daphne cause to smile. 'One down. Two to go.' The coin wavered on its spin. 'They told me, the old ladies... the sisters, they said that demons don't die. Where do they go?'

'Buggered if I know. Now, any questions?'

Daphne did have a question, one that had been burning in her for a while. 'The mannequins. It's working, isn't it? You're making it work. But not Mum's. Why isn't it working for Mum?'

Agatha Hunter looked genuinely sympathetic. 'My dear, that is a detail I think you would rather not know.' She looked at Daphne, and her face softened a touch as she sighed. 'But if you must,' she said as the door silently opened in the shadows behind her.

The old witch sniffed and her eyebrows dropped a moment before Daphne noticed the deathly smell enter the room.

Downstairs, a young child let out a harsh cry.

Agatha Hunter dropped like a stone, landing hard on her front with a pop of a rib and crack of the skull, everything happening so fast Daphne had barely realised this wasn't part of Agatha's games. The elder's feet had been yanked from under her by an invisible force and she'd landed like a sack of bones slamming onto the floor, apparently stunning her. She looked up at Daphne with a dazed look in her eyes.

Agatha's voice was low but assertive, her face turning from dazed to matter-of-fact. 'Don't run, hide,' she said as she made eye contact with Daphne, half a second before being yanked feet-first out of the room. The sound of her bouncing down the stairs was loud and violent.

Daphne approached the top of the stairs slowly, gripping the metal poker in one hand, fruitlessly flicking the lighter to heat the end. Only small sparks flew. When she got to the top of the stairs and peered down, she saw, at the bottom, nothing but a pile of Mrs Hunter's clothes.

The child's voice from downstairs stopped crying. The house fell into near silence. Nothing moved, aside from the darkness that looked to creep in and around her.

She could see and hear nothing.

Nothing but the sound of the coin, still perpetually spinning on her bedroom desk.

And then, from downstairs, the pitter-patter of tiny feet. The sound of a child, laughing, a deep growl emanating from beneath the laugh.

At the bottom of the stairs stood Daphne's new worst nightmare. Alfie stood, gripping a familiar large knife, a knife from her own kitchen, a knife that never blunted, smiling up the stairs at her.

'Ding, dong, the bitch is dead. So let's do this, Daphne Locke.'

Chapter Twenty-four

DAPHNE RAN BACK INTO her bedroom and slammed the door shut. She twisted the useless flimsy metal lock and braced herself against the door. Little footsteps came closer, up the stairs, along the hall, and stopped right outside.

The tapping on the door came from low down, around her thigh level. But though this demon was in the body of a small child, she knew it was as powerful as the others. Probably more so.

She ran for her laptop and hit the power button. Her last chance now was Olivia, her demon-killer friend. Olivia would rip the demon to pieces in a second. Her messenger page loaded up and she scanned to see Olivia's name. It wasn't there. In place of Olivia's name was simply the words "Inactive User". Olivia had closed her account. She had gone. Daphne was truly alone. Except the message preview from the inactive user was unfamiliar. Daphne clicked and read the last message Olivia had sent to her, desperately hoping it would say something useful. WE BEAT A REAL DEMON, DAPH. TAKING SOME TIME OFF SOCIALS FOR A BIT, NEED TO PROCESS, LET'S HANG OUT SOON X

The latest message sat above Olivia's. It was from Paulie. The preview, she couldn't help but scan, said: TRYING TO CALL, NOT EVEN RINGING. ARE YOU OKAY? WE CAN...

She didn't have time to click and read. Whatever Paulie wanted, it was too late.

The only thing that would happen soon to Daphne was she would die or get possessed by the demon in Alfie. The demon outside her bedroom door.

The voice that shouted at Daphne from inside her own mind was so loud it took her by surprise. *Listen!* It said. *Listen!*

Listen to what? And then it hit her. *Don't run, hide.* Another lesson. Daphne had run. There was nowhere to hide. Under the bed? Under some clothes? They were ludicrous ideas, forming out of desperation to follow the final instructions from Agatha Hunter. *Don't run, hide.*

The lock on her door twisted. The door opened. The possessed child stepped in, smiling.

'They just twist, and then they open. I get let in after a little twist. It's quite straightforward.' The growl under the playful voice of Alfie made Daphne hate the demon even more.

'I will not let you in,' replied Daphne with her last ounce of defiance.

There was nowhere to run or hide. Mrs Hunter's final advice had been useless.

'Then, I shall start the dismembering of the offspring you called Alfie,' said the demon in the child, holding the knife to Alfie's arm and making a small incision. Blood dripped onto the floor.

'No,' said Daphne, desperate not to submit, the hanging noose behind her coming into her awareness.

'The child's blood not good enough for you? For shit's sake ant, why must you be perpetually difficult. Do you not know how fucking annoying it is to inhabit the mind of a child? They just do not shut up. Still, not for long.' The demon boy dropped the knife and waddled over to Daphne's laundry basket and emptied it onto the floor. Then it crouched and made a hole in the middle of the pile, making the shape of a bird's nest. It looked up at Daphne. 'It stinks. It stinks because you stink.' The demon then reached towards the cigarette lighter.

Quick as a flash, Daphne darted forward and grabbed Alfie, wrapping her arms around him and holding on to her elbows so however much he wriggled and struggled – and struggle he did – he would not break free. She wrestled him towards the noose. This was her shot.

Daphne's arms fought hard to contain the child as she positioned herself under the rope and raised the kicking child aloft. The feeling of Alfie's little body was so familiar – she'd picked him up so many times – and though she was filled with anger and fight, aiming his head for the hole in the noose broke her heart.

The demon's fight was strong, and Daphne's arms began to shake. And then the demon stopped struggling, and started to laugh. Daphne couldn't reach. She was too short by just a few inches, and how this amused the demon. She pushed herself up on tiptoes, straining and stretching her arms, and was still a fingernail too short. The boy just laughed some more. The demonic voice disappeared, leaving Alfie's laugh rolling out of the boy's mouth, more and more hysterical every time Daphne tried to hook his neck through the noose, she never quite tall enough, the boy always just a little too wriggly and heavy.

Then it happened. The forehead slipped through, then the nose followed. Daphne's spark of hope was doused when the child unleashed a bladder-load of urine, which flowed down under the army trousers and cascaded down onto Daphne's face. As she recoiled, she pulled the child back away from the loop.

'Put me down, pissy-face,' it said, a growl returning under the child's voice, before a demonic leg extended from Alfie's and kicked Daphne in the face, cracking her nose and sending her flying backwards onto the carpet.

The child tumbled out of Daphne's arms and executed a perfect forward roll, springing back up like a gymnast, chest out, hands in the air. It snatched the lighter from the floating tabletop and skipped back to the nest of clothes, broke off the top with its bare teeth, and poured the contents onto the clothes. And poured, and poured. The liquid did not stop coming. Mrs Hunter's tiny lighter held enough liquid to drench the entire pile of clothes.

Daphne watched in desperation, searching for ideas but her mind unable to function, her nose bleeding and head ringing from the demon's brutal kick, her face now covered in a mix of blood, tears and demon piss.

The demon in Alfie's body hopped into the middle of the pile of clothes and plonked down, cross-legged, nestled in the middle. It held the lighter high and sparked a flame. 'I can escape the moment the liquid is lit. The child will endure a death more painful than his last, revived to mortal life by me just to die painfully once more. You will burn to death. Your house will be rubble. Your choice now, Daphne ant.'

The demon began to lower the hand holding the flame, slowly, smoothly, never breaking eye contact, never dropping its grin.

The reality of the situation smacked Daphne in the face and the gut, and her own voice shouted at her loudly from within. *STOP!*

That was the very moment Daphne knew she had finally lost. She was hopeless and helpless. Out of options. The only way to get the demon out of him was to let it into her. Otherwise, Alfie would burn, as would she.

Daphne collapsed sideways onto the floor. And as she fell, so too did the coin. Daphne listened to the whirring slow as it rolled on its circumference, near horizontal on the table, before she heard its final *clink*, signalling the end of its taunting. The magic was over.

The possessed child scrambled from the pile of clothes and stood on tiptoes to see the coin. 'I'm guessing tails means you're a moronic worthless shit.'

Tails. *Revenge.* How utterly ridiculous. No, the coin finally giving up and falling was giving her a message. Time for her to give up, too. She had failed. *I'm so sorry, Alfie. I'm so sorry, Sara. I'm so... stupid.* Thoughts went from sorry to worse, bringing more pain with each one. *I've failed you both. I've failed you, sisters. I'm so sorry, Mum.* She cried and wailed on the floor, and when she caught her breath, all she could hear was the demon laughing, a disgusting blend of a child's mocking giggle and low-pitched rumble.

Daphne screamed. 'I'm out! Do what you're going to do. You've won, you fucks. You fucking fucks!' Daphne was distraught as she lay slumped on the floor, looking up at the child with the demon inside it, so sorry for her failure as it approached her slowly, flaming lighter in hand, step by step, smiling, standing over her.

'Answer me one question before you do this,' said Daphne.

'Go on,' the child said as a huge yawn poured out, the child's voice missing, leaving just the rumbling growl.

'Which one of you killed Mum? Was it her? The one in Mrs Legge?'

'Oh that,' said the demon. 'Yes, that would be the one with the worm who looks like her. Not I. Not I.' The demon in the child's body did a little tap dance, threw out its jazz hands, and said with a grin and a wink, 'I just ate her.'

Daphne wasn't bothered by the silly dance. Just knowing which one had killed her mother felt like some kind of consolation. A last, infinitesimally small victory. She'd lost, and now she would be dying too. Not only dying, but losing everything and risking the whole world, too.

Daphne Locke, the night witch. *Sorry, Gugwana.*

Tears poured down Daphne's piss- and blood-stained cheeks. The demon eyeballed her and raised the lighter in the air. It extinguished the flame with a dramatic puff of air, like a fire eater in a circus blowing out its torch, and released its grip on the lighter. It finished its cartoonish performance with a flourish of the fingers and a silent *ooohaaah* of the lips, a magician showing empty hands. Eyes still fixed on Daphne, the demon's real head seeped out from Alfie's, and a huge, scaled foot stepped forward from within the child's body.

'Leave, now, make room for me,' growled the demon, its huge form towering above her as Alfie's body lay panting on the carpet behind it. 'Move aside.'

'I'm sorry, Mum,' were Daphne's last words before she felt her eyes close and her consciousness steadily start to leave her head. She was watching herself as if from above. Just like in her flashbacks. Just like when she had attacked her boyfriend. Except this time felt different. This time she was really leaving.

She had no choice but to let the demon in.

As she squeezed her eyes shut and smelled the stench grow stronger, something physical, something with the smell, the taste of death, slimily pushed through her lips. It was entering her. And Daphne had no fight left.

It was time to let it in.

Chapter Twenty-Five

THE CHILD'S VOICE FROM inside whispered so loud it pulled Daphne's consciousness back to self-awareness just before she had fully left her head. *Listen!* It screamed. *Listen to her!*

Listen? Listen to who? Listen to what?

Don't run, hide.

And then it clicked. It took all of the last of Daphne's strength to pull herself back into the depths of her mind, where the demon had now almost fully entered through her mouth.

And there she was. Daphne, in the depths of her mind. The darkest corners, where she had not been since she was a child, except for in her nightmares. And there, in the darkest far corner of her mind, she hid.

It was better than running, apparently.

She could feel the demon entering, taking control. And as she hid, she relinquished control of her body.

When she opened her eyes, the landscape she now crouched in was not her bedroom, or anywhere remotely like it. She was somewhere bigger but smaller. Somewhere familiar but new. Dreamlike but real. Scary yet safe.

✷ ✷ ✷ ✷ ✷

A landscape of memories, happy and sad, inside and outside, real and imaginary, all at once. Above, no ceiling nor sky.

The entire view above: a giant dome, filled completely with hundreds, thousands of giant seats, and on those giant seats, the huge faces of humanlike giant ants staring down. A thousand ant heads of blacks and browns and blues. Short antennae and long. Each unique yet the same. So huge and distant yet clear. Not one with an expression beyond neutral, matter-of-fact, inquisitive, watching intently without a blink amongst them.

They had watched her let a demon in.

And then, her eyes, her other eyes, her real eyes made of water and flesh, opened, now what her brain could see was clear. Her body, Daphne's humanlike body of flesh was moving. Standing. Looking around her bedroom, the demon in control of her body. The vision through her eyes approached a mirror and looked in. The shadows inside so dark and numerous, better to hide in these shadows.

Through the huge windows of her human eyes, from the vantage point in the darkness, in clear pictures: the demon in Daphne's skin stalking through her room. Her hands of flesh opened her wardrobe and she watched her fingers skim through the clothes. The top her mother had given her one Christmas. The pink shirt she wore the first time she met Paulie. Next, the dressing table, where the hands grabbed her make-up, each pot being brought close to the windows of her eyes, inspected. Back to the wardrobe. Daphne's shortest skirt, one she had bought as a Halloween costume but had never had the guts to wear. It dropped the belt-like skirt on the bed, and then the sound of her own voice echoed through her bedroom and beyond and within.

'Breedy breedy ant time,' the demon voice said. Her hands pulled a skimpy, over-revealing top from a hanger. She recognised it instantly. She'd never had the confidence to wear that one either.

She watched from her vantage point in the shadows of her mind as her body moved across the bedroom and picked up her laptop.

'Breedy breedy time.' That creepy low voice.

She watched her own hands and fingers type into the browser, calling up a taxi firm. She watched as the words landed on the screen. Two Hanging Hill Lane. Then the next box. The destination: Club Angel.

Shit.

Club Angel. A dive of a nightclub, a known stop-off for anyone wanting easy company for the night.

'Breedy breedy,' came the voice again, and sickness rose to and through where her stomach would be, if it was still hers. The hands in front of her typed in the order time.

Twenty minutes. In twenty minutes, she would be in a taxi on the way to a horrible bar in her tiniest skirt and top, the demon looking to breed its night witch.

The hands typed in the name. Daphne.

Her hands clicked the order button.

'Breedy breedy time,' a voice said again, this one sounding just like Daphne.

Its plan was clear. Breed Daphne. The ant will release its spores. The landscape all around changed to reds and gloopy purples and colours of disgust.

And then, in the dark depths, from the corner of her mind's eye: a child running away.

A child with a stick.

Another child with another stick.

Except this time, it was not a local celebrity missing child. It was not the neighbour's kid.

She was a majorette. She was scared.

She was Daphne.

Chapter Twenty-six

THE CHILD LOOKED BACK at Daphne, turned, and ran into the dark blur behind her. Daphne followed as quietly as she could. She looked up to the vast dome of ants above her, all looking straight at her. None made any expression at all.

She was getting the definite feeling they were there to judge.

One ant's mouth twitched and fell still again.

The child stopped, turned to her, and said in a soft whisper, 'Come.' She spun around and ran into the shadows, and Daphne followed.

The child had gone. There was nothing but darkness, tinted with an ever-changing subtle colour, sometimes taking shapes, sometimes speckles, and sometimes not there at all, and a sky built of judging giant ants above two giant windows, through which she could see the world she had lived in until now. The child appeared from the shadows and grabbed Daphne's hand, forcing from her a jump and a yelp. They both stopped, Daphne's hand over her mouth. She looked at the windows of her human eyes. They had stopped moving, and defocused.

The child looked up at Daphne. 'Oops. She knows you're in here now.'

Fear shot through Daphne, and the child gripped her hand and started to run.

'This way, come, quick,' said the child.

'Where are we going?' said Daphne as they ran.

'To rescue them. They are waiting.'

'Who?'

'Shhh, run.'

'Locke!' The voice boomed through the world around her, a thick, wet, guttural voice that sounded like it came from all directions at once, yet directed straight at her.

'She's coming,' said the child in a panic before disappearing off into the bending mist and shadows.

And Daphne was alone, and everything around her disintegrated into darkness, and the ants above stared down. And then she felt it under her foot.

The knobble.

An escape hatch, perhaps. She reached down and the handle revealed itself, and she grabbed the metal and pulled and yanked but it did not open.

'Locke!' boomed the voice from closer this time as the child ran across the darkness in front of her.

'She's coming,' said the young majorette, and Daphne chased the girl through the darkness, only to find herself surrounded by blackness, and judging ants above. And then, under her foot, she felt a bump again.

The knobble.

She crouched down and the handle presented itself again, and she yanked and pulled and nothing gave, and then the big voice boomed louder and closer.

'Locke!' So close now.

And the child ran across through the dark with her stick. 'She's coming,' she said and disappeared into the darkness as Daphne gave chase, finding herself surrounded again by nothing but mist and darkness and a giant dome of judging ants looking down on her, and she was alone and lost with nothing around her.

And then, under her foot, she felt it.

The knobble.

She reached down and grabbed the handle and yanked and pulled, and without warning the metal crumbled and broke off in her hand and the metal disintegrated and fell away, and the knobble was dust and no more.

'She's coming.' The words echoed around her mind as she fell into a panic, wondering if this quickening but never-ending loop might trap her for eternity, her version of Hell, panic, the knobble, 'She's coming,' panic, the knobble, 'She's coming,' and the knobble disintegrated again. Round and round she went. 'She's coming.' The knobble. Dust.

'Locke!' bellowed the voice, now inches away. Daphne turned, hoping to see something, anything but darkness and the prison that had closed around her in an endless loop. And there she was. The demon. She had found her.

'You hide here, Daphne ant. You are the most stupid ant I have found in a thousand centuries. You have chosen eternal torture. You have chosen to witness and feel all I do with your body. You have chosen to experience it all. And there is nothing you can do.'

The demon put out a clawed hand and gripped Daphne by the neck, raising her up, tipping her head back. A thousand ant faces looked down, judging her failure matter-of-factly, watching intently. And then the demon squeezed and Daphne thought she could feel the life force draining from her. It let go, and Daphne fell.

'I will not kill you. You will stay. You are powerless. You can but watch. I will play with your body out there, and your mind in here. Enjoy your stay, watching, crying, losing, wishing you were dead, wishing all would end. I will enjoy your pain, it will help me feed. You will see everything. You will feel everything. And now, the time is almost upon us. Enjoy the show, Daphne ant.'

The demon looked so powerful. So utterly unbeatable. She had made a huge mistake staying here. 'What show?'

The demon leaned in, close, closer, so close it might have reached right inside her mind all over again. And the beast smiled, and it spoke, and all was disgusting, sloppy thick tones.

'Breedy, breedy.'

It pointed at the huge round windows that opened, gateways to the real world, where Daphne's face was looking in the mirror applying bright red lipstick. She already had on long lashes and thick black eyeliner. 'Woah, Daphne ant,' said the demon's guttural voice. 'You're hot.

Gonna get it, Daphne. Gonna find you a desperate old stinking fatty for some breedy breedy.'

Daphne was as sickened as she was scared. The demon rubbed its powerful hands together and walked off into the darkness. Before it slipped into the shadow it stopped, turned, and said, 'Don't go anywhere. And should you start to cry, then that shall go on for an eternity.' It laughed and disappeared.

Daphne fought the urge to cry. She knew the demon was probably right, and she was not going to let herself into an eternity of despair. And yet she had no way to fight back. No way to stop it.

Something glistened and stepped through the smoke and shadow. The child. Young Daphne.

'Is it gone?'

Daphne paused, unsure.

'I think it's gone. Follow,' the majorette said.

The child led Daphne through the shadows and the landscape turned to morphing memories which changed as abruptly as a dream. One minute she was running through the Old Gallows Pub and the next through her school, her old high street and jumping over her mother's bed. It made no sense, and all the while, a thousand straight-faced ants stared down at her.

The child stopped. 'We're here.'

'Where?'

'Over there.'

And then they were over there, on the other side of the shadows. And ahead, in the dark, was a rusty cage. Inside the cage, something moved. In the sky, all was still and watching.

'Who is there?' asked Daphne.

'I'm small so I got out. The cages can't keep a child in.'

'Who is it?'

'They. You mean they.'

The child was right. Behind the cage was another cage, and behind that, another.

'Who are they?' whispered Daphne.

'You know,' said the child. 'It's the exiles. Come. Come.'

Daphne approached the cage and saw the woman inside. She looked up at Daphne. It looked just like her. Except this was different. This woman was angry. She was furious. Almost feral. Strong. And she looked like she could handle anything.

The woman whispered with determination, 'Let me out. Let me join you.'

The voice was so familiar. It was the voice that had been whispering at her to listen, to follow the advice of Mrs Hunter, but it was so much more. It was *so* familiar. It was the voice that had come to her in times of need and helped her be strong, the voice that told her all her life she would never be beaten. It was like meeting an old friend. Daphne grabbed the cage door, and yanked. It didn't open. She yanked harder and harder. It didn't open, and a rattling sound echoed around Daphne's mind, and Daphne felt the demon move around somewhere else both far away and close. It was in there with her, somewhere, up to god knows what.

'Psst,' said another voice. 'Let me out.'

Daphne approached the next cage. This time, Daphne wasn't inside. She looked at the old woman in the bars, and held back the tears, her hands flying onto her face, cupping her mouth.

Her mother looked back and gestured for her not to let herself cry. 'She'll hear you. And then you'll never stop. Stop, please; she'll hear you.'

Daphne couldn't stop, and could feel the demon drawing nearer. 'Is it really you?'

The woman's eyes glinted. 'Yes, and no.'

Daphne's cries tried harder to emerge, the sobs trying to force through.

'Let me out,' said her mother. 'You don't need her anymore.'

'Who?'

'Her. Look around.'

Daphne looked around and there was just mist and darkness and a sea of ant faces above and two giant windows showing a mirror, in which Daphne's human body was putting in two large hoop earrings. 'Who put you in here?' Daphne said to her mother.

The feral woman in the cage moved over into a kaleidoscopic light. She moved like a soldier, her arms hard, her face serious yet relaxed as she stared at Daphne.

'You did.'

Chapter Twenty-seven

'LET ME OUT,' MARTHA Locke said to Daphne again. She looked exactly as she always had. Short, rotund, mischievous, loving. She was the mother she had loved and missed so much.

Daphne grabbed the cage doors and yanked and pulled and the cage rattled, but the door didn't budge. The harder Daphne tried, the more futile it all felt and she felt panic rise. She was so close to everything she had wanted, yet seemed to get further away with every hard yank and pull.

'I don't know how,' Daphne sobbed.

The hardened woman – still Daphne but without the constant subtle look of anxiety – stood silently by her cage door, watching. The majorette stepped next to Daphne.

'You have to let them out,' said the child.

Daphne saw the pained expression on the child's face, and crouched down. Eye to eye they stared at each other,

Daphne as a young adult and Daphne as a child, staring into each other's eyes, and they both saw the pain the other held. Daphne pulled the majorette close for a hug, and all felt good and right for the first time in a long time, and the sound of the child's baton landing and rattling on the floor echoed around the giant space, and a demonic laugh rang through the curling mists.

Daphne turned and looked out of the giant windows into the world. There she saw herself in the full-length mirror, wearing more makeup than she had ever worn in her whole life, a little crop top, and a tiny skirt that barely covered her underwear. She hardly recognised herself. She had to do something fast or she would soon be watching herself breed with any disgusting man the demon saw as a fit father to sire a baby.

Daphne tried her best to smile at the young version of herself. 'Don't worry. I'm doing my best, okay?' The child nodded. Daphne picked up the majorette's baton from the floor. But before she handed the stick back, the muscle memory from years before worked some magic, her fingers felt loose and nimble, and the stick twirled perfectly in her hand. It had been a long time since she had last done that. A lifetime. She passed the stick back to the child, and turned to her mother.

'I don't know what to do. What do I do, Mum? Help me, please.'

Her mother stared back.

'You have to let her go. You don't need her anymore.'

Daphne looked at the child, fighting tears, shaking. 'I can't abandon her.'

'Not her,' said her mother. 'Her.' She looked up.

Daphne looked to see where her mother was looking. The ants all looked back. But beyond the mists and darkness all around, Daphne saw a face. It was so big that she'd almost missed it, looking for something small. A face that completely surrounded and encompassed her and everything around her. Her own face. Her own expression she was forever putting on to pretend she wasn't scared. The mask she was putting on every day. The picture of how she *wanted* to be seen, so she wouldn't be laughed at. The face she put on to mask the stupid girl underneath. The face that could turn plain and invisible at a second's notice.

'Her,' said her mother. 'Her.'

'But that's me,' said Daphne.

'It is not. No more than I am, or she,' she said looking at the majorette. 'Or, even, she,' she said, looking across at the Daphne in the cage. 'Now, let her go.'

Daphne felt fear rise inside. 'But I need her,' she replied without thinking.

'You do not.'

'I do.'

'She is the one who is keeping you in here. If you wish to leave, you must let her go.'

'I can't,' said Daphne. 'I'm not ready.'

Her mother stared back with a look of soft love. 'Agatha says otherwise,' she said with a smile. 'And I am inclined to agree.'

Daphne looked up and felt her, felt the huge face of herself that encompassed everything. And then the face turned inwards from all around and looked at her. It looked so scared. The look of fear was so familiar, she'd looked at it in the mirror forever, but until now, she hadn't seen it.

'Don't be afraid,' said her mother. 'She will be happy for you. She is just afraid too. Now, let her go.'

The huge face cried a golden tear, and then surprised Daphne. It gently nodded.

'She has to go,' said Daphne's mother, and the huge face all around nodded again.

The ants stared down, emotionless, judging.

'Okay.' Daphne sank to her knees and put her head in her hands, squeezing her eyes tight shut. 'Okay.'

The giant face all around fell away like the outer layer of an onion, which dissolved into the darkness, and Daphne desperately wanted to cry, and her mother smiled a soft smile before another huge face encompassed all, the next layer of the onion, so scared and shaky, and Daphne knew she had to release her too. And she released her and the face peeled away and her mother smiled a soft smile as another face revealed itself all around her and it was the face of Daphne as she looked at Charl, clothes in her hand, making the decision to swap the clothes that would lead to the death of Sara and all the terrible things that were happening.

'Let her go,' said her mother, and Daphne shook her head.

'No. I'm stupid and I deserve this, look what I did.'

'No,' said her mother.

'No,' said the Daphne in the cage.

'No,' said the majorette.

'That's three against one,' said her mother, and Daphne felt her breath lighten, and the face fell away and dissolved, another layer of the onion gone, and the vision through the windows to the bedroom on planet Earth revealed a clock.

Dong. A woman's voice echoed through the house and the dreamscape around her. 'Taxi to Club Angel.'

'Breedy breedy,' said the huge voice of the demon. 'Let's go and find you a fat old worm. Mmmmm.'

It sounded like it was licking its lips.

Chapter Twenty-eight

'I CAN'T DO IT,' said Daphne, tears starting to feel unavoidable. 'He's going to breed me, and I can't stop it. What have I done?'

'That is as may be,' said her mother, looking at her with great affection and sympathy. 'It is your job to both fight it and accept what is. And what is, is a demon in control of your body.'

'But I don't want it to be!' yelled Daphne, distraught.

The demon voice grunted inside. 'An old, wrinkled, unclean worm, and a young, fertile witch body. Breedy breedy.' The deep, guttural voice crept through the crevices of Daphne's mind and made her want to throw up.

A car engine shook to life in the distant world.

'Help me, Mum. Please.'

'I cannot.'

'But why? You're a witch. You should be able to help me. I need you.'

'I cannot help because I am trapped here, and out there, I am gone. Out there, I am gone. In here, I am trapped. You are not.'

'Mum, listen to me. I want to go. To run away. I don't want to do this anymore. I want to be away from that world, away from the demons.' She stared at her beautiful mother. 'With you again. Is it too late to run away? To just run? I don't want to die.'

'Oh my dear, die you must, in a sense, but not in the one you think of.'

'Stop the riddles, Mum, please!'

'Okay, I shall be clear as a crystal. What were the options you gave to the coin?'

'Heads I would...' She hesitated, weirdly embarrassed. 'Heads I would run. Tails, I would get revenge on all that have wronged us. Kill all the demons. Except I know I'm not strong enough and they'd get me.'

'Oh.'

'Oh?'

'Yes, oh.' Her mother looked confused. 'So why do you think you chose revenge?'

'It landed on tails, and I know I was controlling it.'

'It landed on tails, you say?'

'Yes.' Daphne looked down at her feet and the ground around her swirled.

'Did it?'

'Yes! Why are you being like this?'

'How do you know?'

'The demon told me.' Immediately, she realised her mistake.

'Why do you believe demons but not your own strength from inside?'

Daphne stopped, stunned, and thought back. She hadn't seen the coin land. The demon had told her it had landed on tails, and she had believed it, because a part of her had wanted to.

'My dear you do dally even with your thoughts.'

'It was heads?'

'I do not know and it does not matter. You know what is important to you. But that comes after a fight you must first win, and you are delaying because you are scared.'

Daphne looked up at the huge windows to the world, and sure enough, Club Angel came into view. The neon sign was dirty and the 'G' was out. A man was pissing on the wall next to a young woman who was throwing up.

The bouncers were huge but seemed to do nothing but laugh and smoke.

'You sure you want to do this?' Came a distant female voice. 'You seem like, you know, a nice girl.'

'Fuck off,' came Daphne's voice and the taxi driver through the giant windows looked horrified.

Daphne felt rage and fear rise together. Things now felt different. Like she had permission to get a little reckless. Like she was, for the first time, allowed to put herself in danger and go for blood. It was all or nothing.

A car door thud echoed around the giant space, and bass and drums pounded in the distance.

'You need to stop this, now, daughter.'

'Breedy breedy little one, let your mind and your pants fall all undone.' The horrible omnipresent voice of the demon was mocking. She could almost hear the wet grin. The idea of a fight suddenly felt so sickly sweet.

'Just help me.' Daphne looked up at her mother in the cage. 'I need to know what to do. How do I get out? How do I kill them?'

'Oh they don't die, dear. But you already know how to escape from here. You know that, and you know this: accept what is, Daphne. I cannot help. This one is up to you. And them.' She looked up.

A sky of ants watched down.

'Them?'

'They watch. As do I. As I always will. Yet now we watch you dally.'

Daphne felt something akin to a punch in the gut. Her mother wasn't ever going to come back, however much magic she tried or tea she took to the mannequin in her clothes. Her face dropped and froze.

Her mother nodded. 'You are starting to understand. Some things, all the magic in the world cannot change. I tried. I could not. Do you understand, my dear?'

Daphne nodded. She understood. She didn't want to. She nodded through wet eyes. Eventually, she mustered a few words. 'Am I supposed to say goodbye? Here? Now? In a place I'm not allowed to cry? What do I do?' Daphne screamed. 'Why aren't you helping me?'

Demon laughter echoed.

'You can say goodbye, or you can not. I'll always be here whether you say it or not.'

'But not out there?'

'I live only here now, and will do until the day you die. Do you understand now?'

'Yes.' Daphne nodded and gripped her head in her hands and felt her head drawn down, bending over uncontrollably until her ears were between her knees. Through the gap in her legs, she saw the feral Daphne doing exactly the same thing, a mirror image. They both split straight through the middle and each half of them split into a trillion pieces which swirled up and around and together before the particulate matter drifted into darkness and dissolved away and all that Daphne was disappeared into the light and winds and shadows.

* * * * *

In the darkness, she remained for an eternity. *She*, if there ever was such a thing. Daphne Locke, or whatever that label represented. Whoever she was. For that eternity, she had no idea. And yet, impossibly, eternity ended in an instant.

* * * * *

She awoke to the sound of a beautiful dawn chorus that flashed and ignited and flared through her consciousness, otherworldly birds sang and one of the birds was Paulie for a fleeting moment, and then they all were, all the colourful birds had heads of Paulie and little awkward flapping wings and everything filled with joy before the Paulie-birds flapped and flew away and dissolved into a thousand more colours, replaced by fireworks from another realm that exploded in celebration; every neurone in her brain felt like they did a synchronised, microscopic happy-dance, and happiness flooded through her very being. The cosmic party died the second she opened her eyes and saw the bars. The cage, that now trapped her inside.

She gasped and her eyes darted around trying to work out her surroundings, scanning for danger. In another cage next to her stood her mother. Outside the cage, young Daphne, the majorette, twirled her baton.

'How long was I gone? What has the demon done with my body? Tell me what it did.' The thought of Paulie, the vision of the Paulie-birds stayed with her.

'You were gone no more than the blink of a human eye, my dear,' said her mother.

Relief mixed with confusion shot through her being as she pushed against the side of the cage, and pushed her arms out towards her mother. Her mother came forward in hers and pushed her arms through the bars too. Their fingertips couldn't quite touch. The tiny gap felt like a giant gulf, and the Paulie-birds flew away once more.

'Mum, I'm sorry. I've got us all trapped.'

'Why do you say that, my dear?'

'Because we are.'

'Are we?'

'They're locked shut!'

'Are they?'

'Yes! I tried. I tried so hard. They won't open.'

'Oh my Daphne dear. Have you even tried? Really tried?'

'Yes!'

'You do you, Daphne, but I'm off to deal with that demon. I feel he needs a good and proper kicking.' Daphne's mother flicked a catch, opened the door, and stepped out of the cage.

Daphne's jaw fell. 'How did you do that?'

'Whaaaaat!' The voice of the demon rattled through her.

Daphne's mother smiled. 'Oops. I don't think she wanted me to do that.'

'How did you do it?' asked Daphne, frantically shaking the bars on the cage door. 'Magic? Teach me the magic, quick!'

'Oh, my dear. They open from the inside.'

Daphne was stunned. Only then did she see the simple catch. She flicked it, and the door swung open. She stepped out, mouth still wide, and looked around. Thousands of ant faces watched down from high above. Every time she looked they were exactly the same, yet different. Sometimes so far away, sometimes so close. Sometimes thousands, sometimes hundreds. Always with the same work-like stare.

'Stop!' yelled the voice of the demon. Deep, sloppy tones reverberated loudly around the mindscape.

'I think we've upset her,' said Daphne's mother with a grin.

Daphne looked back, confused. Why was her mother not afraid? 'What do we do? She is coming for us. I can feel her getting closer.'

'Good,' her mother replied with a smile. 'Let's teach her a lesson, wipe off that shit-eating grin.'

'How?'

'This is your mind, dear. You're in charge in here, not her. By the way, the bar's loose. It's coming right off.'

'Bar?'

Daphne's mother glanced at the cage door. Daphne's eyes followed.

'Break a bit off, my dear. You'll need something to knock some teeth out with. I like the idea of the cage bar. It would be somehow poetic.'

Daphne looked at the bars and stopped, still.

'Did you learn nothing from the sisters? From Deanna? From Agatha? We give you all the ways to win, and you dally still, Daphne dear. So, I will guide you further.' Her mother stepped forward towards her, looked her in the eye and gave a soft smile. 'How do you feel?'

'How do I feel?'

'Yes, that's what I said.'

'Scared.'

'You speak out of habit, not from consulting your feelings. Now, stop, listen, and tell me.' Her face looked soft, kind, relaxed. 'How do you feel?'

Daphne stopped. She took a breath. She searched inside. Her mother was right. She felt different. The fear that had always been there for as long as she could remember was gone. Completely gone. Instead, she felt strong, confident, and more than little bit angry.

'Well?'

'I feel angry.'

'And what did I teach you about anger?'

'It's an invitation to act, not my boss. Just an invitation.'

'Right. And do you want to take up that invitation to go and beat the crap out of that fucker of a demon? Knock that grin off its shit-licking face? Or do you want to lock yourself back in that cage and suffer for an eternity?' She raised both eyebrows.

And Daphne felt strong. 'I want to smash its face to pieces.'

'Good,' said Martha Locke with a loving smile. 'She's drawing near, and we must act fast. Look.' She gestured to the windows to the world.

They revealed a bar. The demon was watching a man sitting at the other end. He was around sixty years old, overweight, crap hair like a monk and a toad-like face. Two young women sat beside him in conversation with each other. The man dropped a pill into one of their drinks unnoticed, and took a sip of his own.

'Breedy breedy Daphne. Do you like my seed selection for your insemination?'

Daphne looked in horror as she saw herself stand and walk towards the horrible man. The man looked back, straight down the eyes.

'Hi,' he said with a smarmy drool and a one-sided smile.

'Hi,' came Daphne's voice from afar. 'Nice to meet you. I'm Daphne.'

Chapter Twenty-nine

FOOTSTEPS, LOUDER AND NEARER. The smell of death, stronger. A thousand ants peered down with unchanging expressions.

The majorette ran into the shadows.

'Stay safe!' Daphne called after her.

'She's been doing that for too long,' said her mother, before shouting, 'Give him hell!'

'Mum?' Daphne looked at her through longing and loving eyes.

'Yes, my dear.'

'I don't think you're right. I can bring you back. The mannequins are getting stronger now. Deanna Tamblyn killed a piskie. So whatever happens in here, stay safe. And when we're done, we'll make sure you come back.'

Daphne's mother's wrinkles deepened. 'We'll see. But now is not the time. Right now, I must check on the girl.'

Before Daphne could stop her, her mother disappeared into the wavering shadows after the majorette. And when Daphne turned around, there it was.

The demon.

The massive, massive demon. Scaley. A beast with a horned head and a long, armoured tail. It approached Daphne slowly, a huge, tooth-lined grin on its face. It towered over her by several heads, and then, one more, as another head popped out from the top of its scaley scalp. As it did, a liquid spurted from the orifice from where the new head had come, and the stench of death surrounded her.

'You have chosen this, Daphne Locke. You have chosen an eternity of torture, of feeling the physical pain I will inflict, witnessing the suffering I will so enjoy! You will feel the full pain of spawning my night army, one after the other popping from your weathered crotch until your body can take no more, at which point I will leave you to painfully die. You chose this, Daphne ant, because you are' – a tongue came out from the shit-eating grin and licked its lips – 'stupid. The stupid little single girl, still alone, always alone.'

'How do you feel?' whispered the voice of Daphne's mother through the darkness. And she knew. She felt strong. She felt angry. And she locked her eyes on the demon's grin.

That shit-eating grin.

The demon continued, 'You chose this suffering, Daphne ant. You chose it, and I shall feed off it every minute of every day, basking in your stupidity. Oh,

Daphne ant, you really are pathetic. Now, prepare your-self. It's nearly time for some breedy breedy, worm get greedy.'

Daphne raised the metal bar that she had prised from the cage. She swung. Demon teeth flew from its mouth as its head snapped around, the second head on top swinging around with it. And then the heads turned back to her, and another head popped out from the top, and grinned.

'All great things come in threes, Daphne ant.'

Daphne stared at the stack of three demon heads, each with a different disgusting grin, and saw nothing but tar-gets. So she swung again, knocking the teeth from the small top head.

The expressions on all three faces turned at once. Sud-denly, it was the demon who looked scared. And it turned, and it ran.

Daphne's foot caught something as she tried to give chase. It felt like her feet were nailed to the floor. Two huge, rusty nails penetrated the top of her feet, fastening them to the ground. The moment she saw, the pain spiked through her and she wailed. She stood trapped, in pain, helpless. Stuck to the floor. The demon turned around and grinned.

'Go get him,' came the shimmering whisper of her mother through the darkness.

'I'm nailed down,' Daphne called back.

'No, you're not, you never were, you just thought you were. Go get him. And do not hesitate!'

Daphne braced herself and stepped towards the demon, and the huge nails in her feet turned rough and brown then black, and rusted and crumbled away and her feet moved easily, piles of rusty dust blowing away in a soft wind. Daphne was astonished, and raised a smile along with her metal bar that crashed down again on the demon's top head, sending its whole body to the floor, and wiping off its grin again.

Daphne smiled, a little hopeful now, and raised the bar up high ready for the killer blow. The demon's foot connected with her first, sending her reeling back into the shadows and onto the floor.

The demon turned and fled.

Daphne's mother stepped out from the shadows and effortlessly tripped it with her broomstick and a grin, sending it tumbling to the floor. The majorette appeared, stood over the demon, and whacked it with her baton in all the faces. The top face, the bottom face. On the shins and on the knees, on its knuckles as clawed hands defended toothy heads, over and over again.

The demon wailed, 'Stop it!' and kicked its legs out at the girl, pushing her away, and Daphne got up and approached. The demon got to its feet, and fled into the blurry shadows as the ants watched down silently from above.

'Let's get him,' said Daphne, striding in the direction in which the stupid beast had fled.

'That's my Daphne,' said her mother, and the thousand ants looked down without making an expression or sound.

Daphne glanced up at the huge windows. They were black. They momentarily opened, a blurry extreme close-up of the face of the sexual predator from the club.

They were making out. The demon was on the run but still had full control.

'You know what they say?' The sudden sound was Daphne's outside voice, talking loudly above the music. 'When they say not to take advantage of young girls because they're somebody's daughter?'

The man through the windows looked curious. Sleazy.

Then Daphne's voice spoke again. 'That doesn't apply to me. I am no one's daughter. Not anymore. You're all out of excuses. Now, come here.'

The huge eyelids shut and the windows fell to black, but there was no time for anger. The demon in the shadows was getting away.

Daphne, her mother and the majorette gave chase. Her mother clutched her old wooden broomstick. The majorette held her baton. Daphne held her cage bar ready.

Through the darkness and shadows they ran, through dreams and memories. Memories of the carnival, memories of the six-eight-ten killings, memories of school and learning to swim and meeting Paulie for the first time. Every time Daphne's attention was taken by a memory, the picture vanished and left her in darkness, running forever, an army of silent ants watching down.

Daphne could not tell if a second or a decade had passed since they started the chase, but now, there it was, up ahead. The demon, scaling a high wall, no, a cliff, making a wounded escape. Beyond the top of the cliff face, the huge windows to the world outside: Daphne's body and the man were making their way through the nightclub's fire escape.

Daphne, her mother, and the majorette reached the bottom of the cliff, and some vines grew out from the face as though to give something to hold onto.

'Nice thinking,' said her mother as the majorette started climbing the wall in pursuit.

'You next,' said Daphne, but her mother just stared back. Daphne could tell from her expression that something was wrong. 'Come on Mum, it's getting away.'

'I can't climb that.' Daphne's mother stepped back and looked up. 'There are some places I can't go anymore.'

'Yes, you can. This is my mind, my rules. That's what you said.'

'*Your* rules cannot supersede *the* rules, Daphne. I cannot go there. And now, you must, and fast.'

'We'll find another way.'

'There is no other way.'

'Then I'll stay here with you.'

'The demon will breed you within minutes, Daphne. And then you will be in a worse position than you are now, trust me. The whole world will be. You must go, now. Save her.'

Daphne looked up at the majorette, climbing fast, catching up with the demon. 'Wait!' Daphne yelled up the cliff face.

'I can get it, I'm catching up,' shouted back young Daphne the majorette.

Her mother smiled. 'You always were a stubborn kid. Always went after what you wanted. Right up until that damn carnival.'

'Come with me. That's what I want now.'

'I cannot.' Her mother looked soft, old, accepting. 'She is getting away and you must go, now.'

'I'll come back for you.'

'Daphne this is where it gets complicated. And there is no time to explain. But once you have beaten that demon, you will return to your world, and we may not meet like this again.'

'What do you mean?'

'I hate to be so blunt, my dear, but we have no time. You will be back out there, and I will only be in here.'

'You'll be in here?'

'It's the only place I live now.'

'What does this mean?'

'It means you must go right now, or you will be bred, and your world will end. You must go, now.'

'But... but Mum.'

'I'm sorry. I cannot come with you. Go. Go now, make me proud like you always did.'

'I make you proud?'

'Always. Always then, always in the future. And now. More than ever, now. Fly, Corky, go! I'll stay here, and pop by in your dreams. Now, you're dallying, go!'

Daphne looked up at the child almost upon the demon, and back to her mother. 'Corky?'

'Go!'

'No. Not if you can't come too. How can I learn to be without you when you are supposed to be the one to teach me?'

'Daphne, there is no right way to deal with death. We all just have to make it up as we go along. But if you do not go now he will breed your body, and you do not want that. You will feel everything, *everything*, and I cannot protect you. Go, please.'

'No!'

'Daphne you will not make my grandchildren be night witches. Please, go now, dear girl. You must go now.'

Daphne looked up at the demon, nearing the top of the cliff, the majorette tailing him, the huge windows to the real world in the background. Outside were two huge bins full of bottles, rubbish strewn all over the floor, and a broom leaning up against a dank concrete wall. It all clicked together: the demon was going to impregnate her between the bins out the back of the seedy nightclub, a final humiliation before she became just a body to breed. She had to move. Daphne hugged her mother, and her arms went straight through her.

'No time for that,' said her mother's voice through the darkness. She was gone and only a shimmering distant voice remained. 'Go, now!'

Daphne grabbed a vine and pulled herself up. She looked up towards the demon, towards the child, and in the background above, a thousand ants watched on.

A blue scratched a shiny, hard head. A red raised an eyebrow.

Daphne climbed fast as the windows to the world revealed Daphne's tiny skirt landing on a pile of empty cans and bottles. The reflection on a discarded piece of glass revealed Daphne's face, smiling, close, and the disgusting man behind her.

Chapter Thirty

DAPHNE PULLED ON THE vines with one arm, pushing with her foot and grabbing the next vine with the same hand. The other hand was busy holding the metal bar that she was going to give that demon a pounding with.

As she accelerated up the cliffside, her arms were strong and her legs were dexterous and nimble. Inside her mind, it seemed there was no muscle fatigue. Just her, and a fleeing demon, and a metal bar. The only complication was the vulnerable majorette, chasing the demon up ahead, and almost reaching it, falling into its trap. That and the imminent disaster between the bins in the real world.

Daphne looked up. The demon disappeared over the top of the clifftop. The child was so close to catching it now.

'Stop, wait!' Daphne shouted at the girl.

'I can get it!' shouted the excited girl as she continued upwards. Above her, the ants watched down.

'Wait, please!' Daphne shouted. But she did not.

Daphne accelerated. Her arms worked fast, her legs pushed hard, and she started to make ground on the child. But not enough. The child reached the top and reached one hand over the clifftop.

'Please, wait one second, I'm coming!'

The child did not wait. The last thing Daphne saw of the child was her little feet disappearing over the cliff edge, joining the demon up there. Somewhere beyond her view.

As though moving as one, the ants all adjusted their gaze to view what was happening on top. Up where Daphne couldn't see. One ant seemed to break whatever the convention was up there and put a tiny ant foot over its mouth, as though it was shocked at what it saw. The ant next to it gave it a glance, and the shocked ant moved its foot and forced its expression to return to a fixed stare.

Daphne raced up the cliffside. Vine after vine rushed down to grab her and pull her up, foot hole after foot hole appeared for her as she propelled herself towards the top.

The vines stopped. She had nowhere to go, stranded halfway up. The face of the cliff started to change in front of her eyes, morphing into something new and different. A face. Features she knew so well. It was her mother's face, looking younger like she remembered her to be as a child, and the face said, 'Grief is like the weather.' And the vines sprouted once more and gave her a way up the cliff again. Almost at the top, the vines stopped emerging, and her mother's face appeared in the cliffside, now looking like the old woman she would never become, and whispered, 'Grief is love.' And the vines sprouted above her once more, and she continued her ascent. When she was in reach, she paused, and took a breath, preparing herself for what she might see. She gripped the iron bar hard and peered over the top.

And there they were.

The demon and the majorette.

And the beating looked utterly brutal.

There was blood everywhere.

The demon was lying on the floor, all three heads squirming, bleeding from holes all over while the majorette stood above, smashing her baton down, hit after hit, strike after strike, stabbing into the fucker's stomach, smashing heads one by one amongst screeches and wails and pleas to stop.

The majorette looked up at Daphne. 'See, I got it!'

'It's a trap,' said Daphne.

The majorette just smiled. 'Better help me hit it then!'

So she did. Daphne piled in with the iron bar, smashing the demon in the face time and time again, each blow making her feel better, stronger, more powerful. She took aim at the little top head, which no longer wore its grin, and smashed it, and smashed it again. She smashed it so hard and so many times that the tiny neck beneath it severed and the head was ready to come right off. The majorette walked over and raised her stick to finish the job.

'Wait!' shouted Daphne. 'Wait. Don't break anything off. I don't want any parts of it staying here. Let's get it out.'

She looked up at the giant windows. Her face now looked down into a bin from waist height, her hands balancing her on the filthy black rim.

Daphne stepped back, and the majorette followed. Daphne blew on the end of her metal bar, which smoked and glowed. 'Get up,' she said, and the demon did, top head flopping and flapping around on its very broken neck. 'That way, towards the windows.'

The demon didn't move, so Daphne forced the glowing end of her stick into the demon's back, where steam hissed off it and the demon trudged forwards towards the huge windows to the outside real world.

'You're lucky I'm not following Agatha's advice, demon,' said Daphne with a grin.

'What's that?' asked the majorette as she whacked the demon in the back the moment it dared to slow.

'Stick the glowing end up its—' She stopped herself in front of the child. 'I'll tell you one day.'

'Up its arse,' said the majorette as she whacked the demon in the back of the knee with a cheeky grin.

The three stood by the giant windows to the world, the demon on the precipice, Daphne standing right behind.

In front of the windows, Daphne's hand came up and turned over, and turned again.

'I'm doing that. I've got my body back.' The sound of Daphne's voice came from outside. She had regained control of her real body and her voice. She was winning – except she could feel two big hands on her waist and a man pressing against her from behind.

The demon laughed. The majorette belted it on the side of the knee.

'You do it, and you will die,' said the demon. 'Out there, I am more powerful than you. So we live in here forever, together, a stalemate. Or you push me out, and I kill you and the boy.'

Daphne manoeuvred the giant window over the bin of broken glass.

'I doubt it,' said Daphne, and whacked it across the back of the head with the glowing cage bar. It fell forward, and a second later, it was on the other side of the giant windows, gasping for breath, flailing around in the bin full of bottles in the back alley of Club Angel.

'Are you going too?' asked the majorette.

'I'm sorry,' said Daphne, 'I really have to go.'

'That's okay,' said the majorette. 'I feel better now.' She smiled, twirled her baton in her fingers, and skipped off into the darkness.

In the bin in front of the giant windows, the demon coughed and slumped down. And above Daphne's head, a sound. She looked up. A single ant began a slow, solitary clap.

And then another joined it.

And then another.

And before long, every ant in the sky was clapping tiny feet.

One even raised its hat.

An iridescent Paulie-bird flew over.

Daphne watched it fly then looked down, feeling something under her foot.

The knobble.

The last thing she saw was a giant image of a coin, tails facing up, before everything went black, and Daphne gasped. The air smelled of stale beer.

* * * * *

When she opened her eyes, she was bent over a bin, desperate for breath, the taste of shit in her mouth, a sexual predator grasping her from behind, and a wounded three-headed demon flailing about in the bottle bin in front of her, catching its breath, balling its fists, its top head visibly healing by the second.

Daphne stood up, elbowing the man hard as she could, forcing him away. She turned to see him, standing naked and miniature-dicked under his overhanging gut, a look of total shock on his face, staring straight past her. Daphne looked around at the demon, then at the pervert, and wondered for a moment which was really the biggest pile of shit.

'And that's why drugging people isn't funny. Don't like it when it happens to you, do you? Now fuck off.'

The man ran away down the dark alleyway, completely naked aside from some thick white socks, his droopy dimpled buttocks reflecting the dim lamp light as they wobbled and bounced. Daphne was sure she heard him start to cry. Then she turned to face the demon, and it was her turn to smile.

Part 3

Demons all the way down

Chapter Thirty-one

WITHIN SECONDS, THE DEMON stood stronger, bigger, and hellishly angry. It would be back to its huge and terrifying self in seconds.

Daphne did not hesitate. She grabbed the broom from against the wall and snapped the wood in two over her knee, throwing down the bristles and gripping the long end, her fingers twitching. As she raised it, the end sparked and smoked, a wisp, a puff, and a glow of red emerged and built, a tear fell from her eye, and the words her tongue and lips formed took her by surprise as she shouted, 'I am still a daughter!' Daphne thrust the fiery stick into the side of the demon's biggest head. The shriek was deafening as fiery wood boiled the insides of the demon's head, squirting out boiling blood onto the bottles and cans. She yanked it out and aimed again, plunging it through its eye.

Daphne's shout matched the loudness of the demon's final shriek. 'That's from a fire ant, you fucker. You lost. You lost and I won. Now fuck off to wherever you fuck off to. Die!'

As the demon's shriek faded, so too did its physical form, and the traces of blood that surrounded it, and the red on the wooden pole subsided and Daphne felt the temperature drop back to something more normal. She reached down and picked up her skirt. It felt so small as she slipped it on and thought of her mother, hoping she somehow was able to witness that from wherever she now existed.

'Two down. One to go.'

All great pricks die in threes.

She wasn't sure if that was her own voice or her mother's.

✳ ✳ ✳ ✳ ✳

Daphne raced home in the first taxi she could find and ran upstairs into her room.

Alfie was gone.

She bolted into her mother's room, and there he was, on the floor surrounded by mannequins, a look of terror on his face. She crouched with Alfie, a crying and mumbling wreck on the floor. He seemed in fine physical shape, but she hadn't seen him look so scared before, and could see the pain and shock in his eyes. She had to stop it, urgently. She had to purge Alfie's memories of the demon inside him and all he may have been aware of. So she did what she had learned to do, stared into his eyes, and drew out the memories. Again, they flowed out as though on tiny photographs: a blurry deserted room and a cry for mama; *yum yum, snack, sharp, Mummy it hurts!* The sight of the demon gouging out the mortuary worker's eyes and pushing in the hooks. Each landed on the carpet and dissolved in tiny puffs of smoke which fizzled away into the air.

When she was finished, Alfie wore a look that had become so familiar to her. On the women on the beach, on Penelope Pengilly, on Doctor Bohn. This was good. He would be fine in three days. She hugged Alfie tight, relief flowing through her, and, without warning or expectation, balled her eyes out. She backed her face away and studied little Alfie. He would be just fine.

But now, the urge to get to work on her revenge had hit a problem. She had a two-year-old child to care for, and nowhere to take him. She couldn't leave him. She needed a babysitter. Or his mother. His mother was, of course, standing above them in plastic form.

Gugwana glowed suddenly with a bright smile, and the mannequin in Sara's clothes seemed to look brighter. There was some shading in the eyes and stubble on the plastic scalp. Daphne's chest felt lighter. Sara's mannequin was most definitely changing. She could put this right.

'Can I leave him with you ladies?' Daphne asked, not sure if or how a reply might come.

The mannequin in Morwenna Rowe's clothes pushed out a hand and raised a thumb.

Daphne had her babysitters. Looking at the mannequin in Sara's clothes, it struck her: she had saved Alfie, and Sara would be so proud. And Mrs Hunter. And her own mother, too. They'd all be so proud. She allowed herself a smile but not to wallow; now she needed to gather weapons, get some sort of plan together, and to violently kill all that had hurt her.

As though she could read her mind, the mannequin in Gugwana's clothes pushed its arms slightly to the side, revealing the catch to her belt and her knife. Daphne couldn't remember where she'd left that knife, and now the ornate blade was back on Gugwana. These ladies really were regaining their powers. Their lives. Daphne unbuckled the belt, and as it fell, caught it, taking the extra weight of the beautiful blade it holstered. She clutched it tightly and looked up at the mannequins.

'I know you're still a bit stiff, but if you can, see if you can magic him up some less ridiculous clothes.' She walked over to the window and looked out. Darkness had fallen. Something moved in the shadows. Daphne's tone changed as her mind returned to revenge. 'As soon as the sun comes up and they can't cower in the shadows. One by one.'

Daphne grabbed some paper from her mother's bedside table. It was time to write a list of all those who deserved her revenge. Charl would be on it. The bean-nighe. The demon who had killed her mother. She looked around for a pen, but couldn't find one. She opened her mother's bedside drawer, something she had never done since she had died. It was empty. She moved around to the other side, and opened it. There was something else that took her attention.

A key.

A small padlock key. She had only ever seen one padlock in the house.

It was under the carpet in the lounge on the handle to the basement.

The knobble.

She had the key to the final secret of her childhood home, the basement. Before getting some sleep, before her mission into the woods at sunrise, she'd let her curiosity win this time. The basement somehow had a draw on her. It was the thing behind the knobble, her last childhood comfort. The basement.

The basement that goes, as Sara had told her, *all the way down*.

✶ ✶ ✶ ✶ ✶

In her haste, Daphne almost tripped over the pile of clothes that belonged to Agatha Hunter. She picked them up, and as she crouched, noticed her own clothing. The tiny skirt showed her pale, scabbed knees and thin thighs. She went straight back upstairs, dropped Mrs Hunter's clothes on her bed, and changed into something loose and comfortable for the evening. She took off the hoop earrings and tossed them into the bin. One more night of relative comfort. The house would protect her for one more night before she would end this.

Downstairs, the knobble felt good under Daphne's foot. She rolled back the carpet again, revealing the dusty old floorboards, the outline of the hatch of the cellar, and then, finally, the old metal handle and padlock. The thing that, along with the carpet directly on top of it, had made up the knobble.

She pushed the key into the padlock and twisted.

Click.

The lock opened immediately and easily. The hatch was unlocked.

Daphne knew she wouldn't be going down there. If the hole was as deep as Sara's, one slip and she may never return. But she could look, and see what might be down there. Look for some clues or secrets of her family's past. There was something down there. Something important. She felt sure of it.

She gripped the handle and pulled. The metal was stuck. She pulled harder and gave a good, hard yank. Dust flew and the hatch rose just an inch or so, and then dropped back down, blowing more dust around the room, getting in her eyes and throat and making her cough. She'd done it. She now just needed to pull it open.

She got to her feet and pulled hard, opening it the whole way, upright, and dropped the heavy hatch back on the floor behind it where it landed with a bang. She knelt over the hole. It was as deep as the eye could see, nothing but blackness, stillness. A light. She needed a light.

And then, from deep down in the dark and shadows as a deathly smell rose with the smell from the depths, a sound.

Dink. Dink. Dink.

A long, low growl, somewhere between a giant animal purr and the enormous, aggressive belch of a giant.

The stench grew stronger and the sound grew louder, clearer, scratching and banging followed. Louder, clearer, nearer. Something was down there and getting closer fast. Before she had a chance to think, something down there moved, heading towards the light of the lounge, and she raced to the heavy hatch, heaved it from the floor, and slammed it shut.

It didn't shut. Not fully. Something was wedged between door and floor. A huge clawed hand. A demon limb. It was a demon down there. And that hand was bigger than any of the hands on any other demon she had seen. The forearm alone was the thickness of a tree trunk, the claws a full foot long with jagged sharp ends that scratched the floorboards leaving deep marks.

She stamped on the hatch door, desperately hoping the hand would withdraw and the demon would disappear back into the cellar. But it didn't. Instead, the door opened slowly. Daphne stamped and jumped on top of it, and another huge hand came out. And then another. And another.

The door lifted higher and a chilling head emerged, then *bang*, the creature smashed the hatch wide open and Daphne against the wall, and the huge beast hauled itself out of the cellar.

It raised itself up, crouched under the ceiling it could barely fit under, and stared at Daphne and smiled. The demon was massive, towering above her, the biggest she had seen.

Fuck.

Daphne stared back. This one was familiar. Familiar from a long time ago.

She pulled the knife from its sheath, and the demon laughed at her. A chiding, mocking laugh that was as familiar as its face. The demon turned, still laughing, and squeezed out through her lounge door. Daphne followed the laughing demon. It made no sense that it was fleeing. It ran straight through her front door, knocking the heavy wood from its hinges onto the small garden outside. It turned and laughed again, then ran briskly into Hanging Hill Woods.

A noise came from the lounge. A hiss. Another demon.

Daphne ran back in. The cellar was still open and hisses and roars and bangs were coming from the hole. She slammed the door down, again catching another clawed hand that was trying to crawl out. More hands reached through the gap between hatch and floorboards. Different hands. Different colours, different sizes, different claws and nails. Scabbed skin to scum-coated scale to scratched bare bone. This wasn't one demon, this was many. And the voices, so many evil voices, came chittering and growling through the gap. She stabbed the knife into a scummy hand, then took the blade out to stab again, and the hand slipped back into the cellar. She stabbed another hand, then another, each hand withdrawing into the hole after the knife had been withdrawn. One scaley hand refused to back into the hole so she stabbed and stabbed again, and when eight long fingers still grabbed at her, she cut it off at the wrist. She stabbed and stabbed until the hands stopped coming and the door finally fell neatly back into place, and all the voices stopped. Daphne grabbed the padlock and slid it through its hole. The noises stopped. The whole house felt still and quiet. *Click*. The lock would have to hold them as it had done for years.

WTF, Mum?

Daphne rolled the carpet back over the hatch, caught her breath, leaned against the wall, and looked at the demon hand that lay by the hatch as the fingers disappeared and the palm dried into a hard leather which promptly turned to dust.

'Shit,' she said out loud. 'That's demons in there. There's demons all the way down.'

Chapter Thirty-two

DAPHNE HAD LOST HER cover of daylight. She couldn't wait for the sun to rise now she had no front door, and at any second, all the demons, piskies and any other creatures from her textbooks could pour in. She could wait in the house if she wanted to, but what for? The house held nothing for her anymore. Not even a front door to protect her. Everything from the entire ground floor of the house – as well as the upstairs bathroom and hallways – the piskies had taken.

She went back up to her mother's room and grabbed the paper and pen from the drawer where she had found the key.

Charl. Gordon Bright. Bean-nighe.

They'd be satisfying victims and she would carve them up like meat. They all went on the list.

Then there were the demons. The huge one that had just escaped from her basement and laughed at her as it left. It would have to be killed too. What was until very recently the last demon, the one that inhabited Mrs Legge. The demon who had killed her mother. That one would definitely have to suffer.

Daphne tapped the pen on the paper, thinking back along the horrible recent events, thinking if anyone else needed to join those demons back in hell.

A few piskies, maybe. They'd taken everything from her. Her childhood memories. The scrapbook left to her by her mother that she had only just found. Yes, they deserved it. That would be easy and satisfying.

The list was long, each name on the paper filled her with anger, and she tapped and scraped at each one with her pen.

She made sure Gugwana's knife was safely concealed in her belt and went into her room, emptied her backpack and replaced the contents with the spiked metal bar left in her room by Agatha Hunter. She lay the sharpened broomstick on her bed, ready to grab and use if she had to retreat that far.

The full moon shone through the curtains. She had no time to waste.

She checked on Alfie in her mother's room. The boy was stock still, staring straight forward, holding hands with Deanna Tamblyn's mannequin. She looked at Deanna's plastic face, the eyes looked back. She looked at Alfie.

Maybe she should call him an ambulance or take him somewhere. Deanna Tamblyn's mannequin blinked as Daphne considered the options.

Daphne ordered a taxi anonymously from a private browser from Hanging Hill Woods. When it was due, she would walk Alfie into the road and disappear back inside and not answer the door. The taxi driver would have no choice but to take Alfie away, or call the authorities, and he would be safe. She ordered the taxi for ten minutes' time.

The mannequins stood as statues, each with some life flickering, somehow poised now rather than posed. Gugwana's mannequin had moved and was now standing at the window staring out. Perhaps these ladies could look after Alfie after all.

When she saw Sara's finger extending – her mannequin was changing fast – towards Alfie, she knew what to do. The mannequins would look after him just fine. She hoped.

'I need to go out for a bit.' She didn't know if she would get a response. It was the craziest situation to need a babysitter for. Sara would have laughed, Daphne was sure. She glanced at her plastic friend, desperate to share the laugh with her. She paused to gather her thoughts, crouched down and put her hands on Alfie's shoulders, concerned by the stunned look on his face. She reminded herself he'd be just fine. He would be. Just fine. She hoped.

She cleared her throat. 'Erm, ladies...'

The mannequin arm of Deanna Tamblyn raised, and a plastic thumb raised from that. The whole mannequin crouched and took Alfie by the hand, a reassuring look in her eyes, then reached around and picked him up, plastic legs straightening, then stood stock still with the rest of them, Alfie just hanging in the plastic arms, staring. He'd be fine. Daphne hoped she'd be around to see it, and the thought of seeing Alfie well again filled her heart with hope.

Daphne returned to her room and sat on her bed, taking a moment – her last moment – of rest while she psyched herself up. She picked up Agatha's iron bar and tapped the side of a cold spike in the palm of her hand. She went to the window; the view was the same as it had been every night since she was a child. The edge of the woods she could see felt different now. Darker. Menacing.

The doorbell rang, sending Daphne's heart racing. She pushed herself against her bedroom door, and listened.

Dong.

They were using the doorbell and she didn't even have a front door. They could just stroll in. More mind games.

Dong.

Then, something completely unexpected startled her. A human voice. 'Hello,' it called. 'Taxi.'

It was just the taxi. She'd completely forgotten.

Daphne peered down the stairs and saw that it was, in fact, a man in a taxi driver's uniform. 'One sec,' she called down, and with no reason to stay in the house with no front door that now offered no protection, she grabbed her bag and walked down the stairs with a sense of purpose.

Concern spread over the driver's face. 'You okay?'

'Yeah. I'm good.'

'Town centre, right?'
'Can I change that?'
'Sure, where you wanna go?'
'Gwydhenn, please. The Gwydhenn Centre Psychiatric
Hospital.'

Chapter Thirty-three

DAPHNE WALKED OUT OF her house through where the front door used to protect her from anything. Now, the thick wood lay already rotting and worm-eaten at the edge of the lawn.

She slid into the taxi with her bag and sat in silence, only one thing on her mind.

Making Gordon Bright suffer.

The driver spoke to her in the rear-view mirror. 'Everything okay? Getting a new front door?'

'Yeah,' mumbled Daphne, uninterested in conversation.

The electric taxi pulled away and drove noiselessly up the hill. Daphne knew all too well that the piskies – or anyone else – could now just walk straight into her house. The mannequins would have to look after themselves now.

And Alfie. She'd go back for Alfie soon, and if she didn't make it, someone would surely find him. The sisters would see to that.

The taxi drove past the old familiar sites. The pub where she had first met Paulie. The pretty beer garden where he had shown her how to do a magic trick of making a coin disappear through easy misdirection. Now the thought of Paulie's beautiful nerdiness briefly replaced the hate she held with something that felt more like love. The chip shop where Mrs Legge worked the fish fryers. The hate returned. There were police outside.

The taxi pulled into the car park at the Gwydhenn Centre and the driver looked round to see Daphne already holding out a banknote. 'Have a good night, then.'

'Yeah.'

'You're a chatty one, aren't you?'

Daphne shot back a look that could kill, slammed the door shut, and stalked into reception.

The grumpy woman stared back at her. 'Gordon Bright?'

'Yeah.'

'You know what to do?' She slid the sign-in form under the glass.

'Yeah.'

'Know where he is?'

Daphne didn't respond, just pushed the form back under the glass and turned to face the door.

'You need this,' said the grumpy woman, sliding a lanyard through to Daphne.

'Yeah.' Daphne took the pass and pushed through the doors into the corridor. She barely registered the other people around her. She knew exactly where he would be. At his normal table, at his normal place, being his normal, disgusting self.

He was.

She approached, grabbing an empty chair from another table as she went, and sat down opposite him.

Bright looked up and grinned. 'Again you come. You like me a lot, don't you?'

Daphne's lips returned a fleeting smile, but her eyes shot daggers.

'Come on then, ant. Tell me. How long before you storm out upset and unfulfilled one more time before you learn that this place is not for you. This is my place now. My place here is at the top. I have earned it. Because I hosted him, and he is all.'

'I killed him.'

'You did not.'

Daphne felt the knife under her coat with her fingertips. Temptation to slice him up there and then pushed a smile back into her cheeks. 'Tell me, Gordon—'

'Detective Inspector.'

'Tell me, Detective Inspector Worm.'

Gordon Bright looked angry. 'What?'

'Tell me how you survive here. A speck of your former self. You've lost everything. Your job, your family, any respect you'd earned over the years. Your freedom. You have nothing. Nothing at all.'

'I have everything. I have the memory of being bonded to him, and that makes our bond eternal. His imprint is strong inside my brain. I have the knowledge that we will be reunited. That is worth more than anything earthly, anything... wormly.'

Daphne's grip softened from the knife. 'And if that was taken away? You would have nothing. You would be a pathetic wretch, homeless, friendless, pointless. The true representation of who you truly are.'

'Ant, what you say is not reality. That story may be true or it may be false, but it is not relevant to the world as it is. If he takes decades to return, I will gladly wait.'

'Waiting in your own piss-filled trousers? Because that is what will happen. You will grow old here. He will not return. And you will be nothing.'

'I will be everything. Because he is returning for me. Me! And that is what makes me everything.'

Daphne stared at his peeling, pathetic face, as a plan formed in her mind. Her face softened. A friendly smile landed on her face. She scanned the room, and gestured over a kind-looking support worker. 'Would you mind getting Gordon a cup of tea please?'

'Of course. Would you like one?'

'Yes please, thank you. Extra sugar, please, nice and sweet.' Daphne smiled and the worker disappeared through a door. Bright looked at Daphne.

'Decided to serve me at last, antling? Or are you up to something?'

Daphne just held her grin until the tea arrived.

Bright gulped his, eyeing Daphne the whole time. Daphne sipped hers. Hot and sweet, just like her mother had made it. Not a word was spoken. Bright's teacup clinked as it landed back on the saucer, empty, and Daphne raised her hand again. The support worker walked over.

'Another please. He is thirsty today,' she said with a smile.

'Of course,' she said, and walked away with Bright's cup.

Their eyes remained locked. Daphne maintained her friendly façade, inside knowing that these cups of tea would lead to Bright's downfall. The worker returned with the cup, this time with a biscuit on the saucer, and placed it next to Bright.

'Anything else?'

'No, thank you,' said Daphne. As the support worker turned and left, Daphne reached forward and took the biscuit off of Bright's plate just before his hand reached it. 'Not for you, Gordon,' she said before taking a bite.

Bright picked up the tea. 'What are you going to do, worm? Try to drown me with tea? That's the thing about women. Obsessed with drinking tea. That, and my phallus.'

'I'm going to destroy you,' Daphne said quietly, before popping the rest of the biscuit into her mouth, chewing it without breaking eye contact, and sipping the last of her own drink. 'Drink up.'

Bright defiantly held eye contact while he guzzled the entire cup in one go, and placed it back on the table. 'I am not scared of tea, Daphne ant. Whatever you have read on the matter, you are mistaken.

'Well then, would you like another?' Daphne challenged.

'As you please,' replied Bright firmly, raising a hand and beckoning another worker. 'Would you mind refilling this, love? Ta very much.'

The worker took the mug and left.

Bright smiled. 'Are we just going to drink tea all day? Is that your plan to defeat me? That's what all the bitch PCs did in the force too. Tried to beat the bad guys by sitting around drinking tea. Took a man to do the job. And here I am again, drinking tea because a pointless bitch can't catch the bad guy.'

The next cup arrived and the worker departed, leaving the tea in Bright's hand. Daphne smiled and spoke softly. 'You will never see him again. You are nothing. And soon, you will experience being nothing. A sad and lonely nothing. Disgraced, a weirdo, living a life of pain.'

'There is no pain where he once was,' Bright said confidently, shaking his head. 'Unfathomable.'

'Shame,' said Daphne before returning to silence. She sat for a further ten minutes, Bright sipping his tea, neither backing down.

'Well,' Bright eventually said. 'I would love to continue this pathetic staring contest, but I loathe to say I still have the body of a worm and still have wormly functions to attend to.'

Bright stood up and headed into the corridor. The door closed. Daphne followed.

When she stepped through the door, Bright was gone.

The plan was working.

Taking the metal bar from her bag, she pushed through the door into the gents' toilets and saw him alone by the wall, singing as he pissed, deliberately missing the urinal. Daphne crept up and cracked him hard in the ankle. He fell to the floor, urine pooling around him. Daphne crouched by his head as he clutched his ankle. She listened for movement outside. Silent and still.

'Say goodbye to him, Detective Inspector,' she said, before cradling his head in her arms and immediately beginning the magic she had practised on Doctor Bohn. They quickly started ejecting from his eyes. Like tiny photographs, memories slid out one by one onto the pissy floor.

Memories of the DI working at the police station, sliding out and disappearing to smoke.

Memories of him fudging records, sending innocent people to prison for cash.

Memories of his first attending Hanging Hill Lane after the murders. Up in smoke.

Memories of meeting the demon. That same demon she had seen before in her bedroom. The demon she had skewered on the sharpened broomstick. The memory disintegrated in a puff of red.

Memories of living with the demon inside his mind. Memories of his beloved demon, landing on the pissy floor, dissolving in his own warm urine, going up in piss-stinking smoke.

Telling Daphne she will burn. Boarding up her house to defeat her. Into the piss.

Begging on his hands and knees for the demon not to leave him, and being laughed at before his beloved master disappeared from his house, followed by three older women sweeping through his house.

The memories kept sliding out, tiny pictures from his eyes to the hard wet floor. His sacking. The press questions. Him being committed to the mental institution. Daphne's visits.

The final picture was of Daphne sitting opposite him drinking a cup of tea. Bright's piss was still pooling all around him, and the last memory fell into the steaming puddle, a tiny whisp of smoke rising from where the image dissolved.

Daphne got up and stood over Bright.

Bright lay on the floor, urine steaming around him, the familiar look of shell shock on his face, lying helpless and wet on the floor of a mental institution bathroom.

Daphne took a moment to appreciate the sight, and the knowledge of what would follow: after three days he would wake up with no memory of the demon that he so adored, or what led him to where he was. He would be a disgraced former policeman with nowhere to go. A miserable wreck of a man. Perhaps when he no longer showed signs of mental issues beyond amnesia, he would be tried for his fraudulent behaviour. Maybe he would go to prison. Maybe he'd be a homeless wreck. He deserved it all. She would enjoy the knowledge of his suffering. She would like that very much.

But for now, the man who had boarded her up in the house with a demon, the man who told her she would burn and that he was glad her mother was dead, the man who had tricked her into questioning the bean-nighe leading to the death of Sara, was lying on the floor, flinching every time she moved, an occasional tear falling and mixing on the old tiled floor in the urine he lay in.

She saw it and it was good.

Before leaving, she would make her innocence known. As she left, she grabbed a support worker. 'Gordon just went to the loo. He said he wasn't feeling well, he looked really quite poorly.' The worker ran towards the toilet as Daphne entered the reception area and slid her lanyard back to the grumpy woman. 'Bitch,' she said to the grump as she left, into the car park and walked hastily away before anyone came asking questions.

The walk back to Hanging Hill Lane and the woods and creatures there was a long one. It would give her time to enjoy the knowledge that Bright would be forever suffering.

As she passed the chippy where Mrs Legge worked, she pulled the list from her pocket, and a pen. She scribbled as she walked, crossing off Gordon Bright from the list. The list still looked long. Two demons. The bean-nighe. The leader of the piskies. And Charl.

Charl.

She would enjoy Charl. He would burn.

Chapter Thirty-four

Daphne passed her own front door with barely a glance. The doorway was wide open, but the door no longer lay on the grass. It was now gone too, likely taken by the pilfering piskies. It didn't matter.

She stalked past what was left of the old stone stack and into the woods, pulling Gugwana's knife from its sheath. She would take delight in slicing up the very next piskie she saw. And if the demons came for her first, she would destroy them too.

The woods didn't look to be in the same beautiful and natural state they normally did. Litter, strewn everywhere. Except, on closer inspection, it wasn't litter. It was Daphne's possessions, broken, torn and scattered all around. She picked up a piece of paper. It had her mother's handwriting on it. Her notebook. They'd ripped apart her notebook. She had to check her anger. She had a job to do. She would use that anger later. Soon.

A small glass pot lay under a hedge. She picked it up. The label now looked dirty, but the writing was still legible. Love salt. The pot was empty, aside for a few specks of white powder inside. Someone somewhere was having a lovely time. Daphne pocketed the container. She now knew that she only needed six granules to make a difference. The residue would account for that.

The further she walked into the woods, the more of her history she saw. Torn pages of the textbooks left to her by her mother. Pots and pans strewn around. A tea-towel high up in a tree.

Her front door in a ditch. The glass of the spyhole glinted in the moonlight.

A voice whistled through the trees. The same horrible voice that had taunted her at the moment of Sara's death. The same horrible word.

'Stuuuuupid.'

The leader of the piskies was near.

Branches cracked and bushes rustled.

The piskies were gathering all around.

Daphne gripped her knife, ready to strike if jumped.

She stopped in a clearing, her back pressed against a tree. A noise from above. Two piskies looked down on her, grinning. Grins which broke into laughs. Worse, the leader of the piskies stepped forward in front of her, dozens of the small creatures behind.

It spoke again. 'Stupid. Stupid, stupid, stupid.' The creature stepped forward, and a spiky ear popped out from under its hat. 'What is that secretly sheathed? A knife, I would guess. To try to stab us all, would be, let's say... stupid?'

Daphne pulled her hands from her pockets and showed they were empty.

The piskie leader smiled again. 'And to come with not even that would be stupider still.'

'I have something for you,' Daphne said. 'Something to buy my freedom. I think you will like it.'

'Go on,' said the piskie leader, and the group above her in the trees cackled and chittered.

She put her hand in her pocket. A group of piskies stepped forward, pulling primitive weapons from their clothes.

'Wait,' Daphne said, pulling her hand from her pocket. She opened it, revealing to them the gold coin. 'Pure gold. And look.' She placed the coin on the open palm of one hand, and spun it with a flick. The coin spun, and spun, never slowing. The piskies looked on in awe. 'It's magic.'

One small voice in the background said, 'I want it.' Several other voices gasped and joined in. 'I want it.' 'It's mine.'

'Quiet!' shouted the head piskie as the coin spun. He stepped forward.

Daphne addressed the leader. 'Pure gold and full of magic. The owner of the coin will be rich forever, and possess the magic in the coin.'

The piskies were getting restless, all stepping forward.

The head piskie put his hand up. 'Stop! It's mine.' The piskies obeyed and stopped, Daphne seeing in their eyes the desperate desire for the coin.

'Come and get it. In exchange for letting me go,' she said.

The piskie leader stepped forward quietly, and stretched out his arm towards the spinning coin.

Daphne grabbed the creature's hand and in one movement, yanked him forward and around, gripping his neck with her right elbow, and dropped down to one knee, holding the coin up in the left hand.

The leader piskie struggled fruitlessly, eyes always on the coin. The other piskies shuffled forward, weapons held aloft.

'It's mine,' one said.

'You want it?' Daphne asked.

A chorus of small voices chittered, 'Yes.'

'Get it.'

She pushed the coin into the leader's mouth and forced it into his throat with her thumb. Even as the creature bit down, she pushed her thumb down into its throat until it choked. As it spluttered, she pulled her hand out, and stepped back. The head piskie looked down at its own stomach.

She stepped away as dozens of piskies piled onto the leader, ripping it apart, desperately searching for the coin.

A coin that was now safely in her pocket. It had been as easy misdirection, and she smiled, feeling a connection with Paulie.

'Stupid,' she muttered, as she stepped away from the frenzied piskies in search of her next victim.

Chapter Thirty-five

WITH THE CHITTERS AND splatters in the distance behind her, Daphne stalked through the woods, knife firmly in hand. A piece of paper flapped on the floor. She picked it up and turned it over. It was a painting she had done as a child for her mother, dirty, torn. She dropped it and continued on her way. Her toaster glistened in the moonlight, abandoned in a bush alongside the spice rack, once beautiful, now smashed to pieces.

Piskie groans came from the distance.

Daphne didn't care in what order her kills came, so she followed the stream down towards the one place where she knew she would find her prey. The old bridge. The home of the bean-nighe. A cardboard box lay on the bank of the stream, soggy and tattered. The pen marking said, simply, "Mum".

Daphne continued down the stream towards the washerwoman's bridge. She stopped dead when a loud crack, a breaking stick, echoed past her from close, very close – and Daphne quietened her breathing as she scanned around. Nothing moved or stirred. All seemed quiet aside from the gentle trickle of the water.

She turned and examined the movements and the shadows, then turned again. Something close had made that crack, and now she couldn't see any sign of anything. Whatever it was felt near, hiding, stalking her. She spun round again, sensing something creeping behind her. There was nothing there. When she turned back around, something flew at her from behind a tree, something long, thin, flying straight at her head. She half-blocked it with her arms before it slapped her in the face, and fell to the floor. An arm. A human arm, blood seeping from the shoulder joint, the fingers still twitching.

Daphne looked up at the tree from where the arm had come, and a foot stepped out. Then the rest of the woman, a woman with one arm, revealed herself with a gleeful smile. The woman wore her mother's clothes; her eyes glowed red, face somehow both glowering and grinning.

Daphne looked at the woman, someone who looked so much like her beloved mother, someone so close to her physically. The dress was the one she had worn when she had received guests. Always that dress. Always on a special occasion. Under the dress, under the skin: the demon inside. Another from her list.

'It's too late,' Daphne said. 'You won't break me. You've failed. You've tried everything. And you lost.'

'No!' roared the demon, striding forward. 'We killed your mother and left her dead in a river. You know that. You... *feel* that. That resplendent feeling of grief and pain and... guilt. Because she died because of you.' It stepped forward again. 'They all died because of you. They're all... *dying*... because of you, because of your decision to resist. Your stupid thinking, that you are more important than they.'

Daphne felt the knife in her hand. It felt lighter, the blade would move fast. Her voice shook as she spoke. 'You failed.'

'Ah, but you do not yet know the details,' said the demon with a grin and another step.

'They don't matter,' said Daphne. 'She's gone.'

'You have learning to do, Daphne ant.' A tentacle shot from Mrs Legge's armless shoulder so fast and with such strength that Daphne didn't have time to react before the slippery limb wrapped around her, slamming her into a tree. A second tentacle fired from the poor woman, and curled itself around a rough trunk. The demon slammed Daphne into the tree and the tentacle wrapped around both. She was stuck and bound. The iron bar in her bag, the knife gripped in her hand, both useless now she was constrained, stuck and braced against the sharp bark.

'So,' said the demon, 'the details of your beloved mother's end. I know you've been dying to know.' Another tentacle left Mrs Legge, then another. The demon's horrific, true face poked out through the woman's stretched mouth, opened its eyes, so many eyes, dozens or more, and stared at Daphne. As it pulled itself from the body of Mrs Legge through her mouth, slime dripped from its chin and scales glistened in the soft light. Two huge legs followed from inside, the feet giant talons. A hybrid of a giant bird or dinosaur and huge sea squid, with the face of a reptile with humanlike features and dozens of eyes, all fixated on her. Its tail was forked. Its colour seemed to be dark blue one second and red the next, but the exact moment the colour changed somehow wasn't perceptible. As the final piece of the creature left Mrs Legge's body, it barked with the rough tonality of a cancerous cough.

'Details, Daphne. Details.'

Mrs Legge stood behind the demon, confused, swaying, mind waking up, dislocated jaw hanging down. Until a tentacle whipped around her neck and squeezed.

Daphne's muscles burst into action but she was trapped, pinned to the tree by something far stronger than she was.

'You see,' hissed the demon, 'your mother didn't beg for mercy. She didn't try to bargain. She didn't even fight me. She just accepted her death like a good little ant. Now, watch my dear, it went a bit like this.'

Daphne stared back at the creature, scanning its crablike eyes, each protruding on a small stalk.

The tentacle lifted Mrs Legge by her neck. Another one slapped her in the face, waking her up.

'Watch, Daphne ant, watch.' Another tentacle whipped around at lightning speed, tearing off one of Mrs Legge's legs which landed in the stream with a splash. Blood poured from the wound, and Daphne gasped as Mrs Legge's eyes widened, horror on her face. 'Look at her face, Daphne ant, look at the pain you cause.'

Mrs Legge was in absolute agony, rendered silent by the tentacle holding her above the ground by her neck. It dropped her in a heap on the floor just for long enough for her to gasp in some air, then yanked her up again.

'Oh, I enjoyed this bit,' said the demon, and plucked the other arm from Mrs Legge, severing it at the shoulder joint and throwing it into the stream. 'I expected her to relent at this point, but she did not. She did not fight nor argue, just as you are not.' It ripped the final limb from the poor woman and fired the leg up into the trees. When what remained of Mrs Legge fainted, the demon's lips elongated, stretching the several feet between it and the poor woman, and breathed into her mouth. Mrs Legge woke up, and the suffering on her face grew. The demon's lips withdrew and it spoke. 'I like to keep them awake so they can suffer. As I did to your stupid shitty mother.'

A tentacle forced its way into Mrs Legge's mouth and pushed in so far Daphne could see the tip wriggling around in her stomach. 'And still,' said the demon, 'she did not submit. So righteous. So pathetic. So... stupid.'

Mrs Legge's face was a dark red, an expression of abject terror as she bled out from where her limbs used to be.

'Enough of this.' The demon dropped the woman, a heap on the woodland floor. 'This is how it all ended for your mother, watch,' it said, and ground her head to a pulp with a tentacle.

Daphne watched, tears falling from her eyes, as the demon scooped up Mrs Legge's lifeless body with a foot and kicked it into the stream.

'Dead in a river, your mother,' said the demon, taking a further step closer to Daphne. 'A river a far bigger than this one. Now, Miss Locke.' The demon paused and seemed to take a breath and savour the air as its many eyes looked at its handiwork in the water. 'Now,' it said, and turned to Daphne, staring into her very soul, and smiled. 'Your turn.'

Chapter Thirty-six

PINNED AGAINST THE TREE by harsh, rugged tentacles, barely able to draw a breath, distraught by the direct reconstruction of the death of her mother by the demon who had actually killed her, Daphne's mind blanked. An immediate flashback hit her: the brutal killing of Mrs Legge, an innocent bystander, and she was unsure if it was mind trickery and she was really watching it again or if it was just in her mind. When the flashback stopped, she found herself completely trapped and helpless.

She'd lost everything. She'd come out to fight, and lost.

'Now,' said the demon. 'As happened to her will happen to you. Limb by limb first, starting with the legs. Until you are nothing but a crying head on a tiny torso, which I will pulp on the ground and toss into the river. Poetic, do you not think? Your mother thought herself a bit of a poet, but I find this better.'

'You won't though, your plan is to take me and you know it.'

'Oh no, not this again,' said the demon. 'That was the plan of some others. I just like to kill.' Dozens of crabby eyes stared at Daphne. 'Did I plan to take your mother? No. I just kill. And I will enjoy killing you as much as I did your mother. Though the worm with the similar features, she was less fun.' The tentacle squeezed harder and Daphne's eyes felt like they were going to pop from her skull as the demon moved towards her, step by step on those massive talons, staring deep into her two eyes with its many. She could see something was different to the other demons that were playing mind games. It was serious. It was going to kill her and laugh as it did. 'You wanted to know why your mother cannot return? That final detail you so crave?' The demon smiled. 'That will be because I ate her heart, as I am about to eat yours.' It wrapped a tentacle around one leg, and Daphne braced her thighs helplessly. 'Your mother, sweet mother. It was not sweet meat but the tough chewiness made it... delectable. A delicacy.'

Daphne squeezed her eyes shut and waited for her body to snap as a vision of the demon eating her mother's heart swamped her mind.

The sharp snapping sound that brought her mind back to reality and echoed through the forest sounded strangely like a trodden-on stick. The *pop* surely wasn't a bone, Daphne felt nothing break. Then another sudden sound: a whip and a crack, a few feet in front of her. She opened her eyes. The demon checked a fresh wound on its head with a clawed hand, and behind it stood a rubbery mannequin with bright red hair, sharp broomstick in plastic hand. The mannequin whacked the demon again, and the tentacle's grip on Daphne loosened. Air returned to her lungs.

The demon turned to face the mannequin, and something else moved in the undergrowth. Another mannequin, this one dressed in brightly coloured clothes, stepped out from the shadows with a smile. It reached out its hand to Daphne's, still gripping the knife despite being pinned to the tree. Plastic Gugwana took the blade from Daphne's hand and approached the demon. Mannequin Morwenna Rowe whacked the demon again with the broomstick. The beast stumbled back, releasing its grip on Daphne further. Plastic Gugwana sliced at the tentacles that held Daphne trapped, again and again, until one fell off and wriggled harmlessly on the ground.

Morwenna Rowe whacked the demon in its cluster of eyes, and it wailed as some fell to the ground.

Gugwana sliced and sliced, and the other tentacle fell, freeing Daphne, who fell to her knees.

The demon screamed and twisted in pain.

'Is this the one?' Gugwana asked. 'That killed your dear mother?'

'Yes,' Daphne said with a grimace. 'And now I am going to kill it.'

'Indeed you are,' Gugwana said with a smile.

Morwenna Rowe cracked it again with the sharp end of her stick. Gugwana punched it in the face and sent it reeling.

Daphne slid the iron bar from her bag.

Morwenna Rowe eyed the weapon approvingly. 'Sister, you've been taking lessons from Agatha, have you not?'

Daphne smiled, stepped forward, and cracked the demon hard on its head. It fell to the floor, writhing in pain, and Daphne kicked it, and kicked it again.

'Mind if we pile on? Seems like a good way to get flexible,' asked Gugwana.

'Don't kill it. It's on my list,' replied Daphne, slamming the bar down as more pieces of demon withdrew into its body.

Gugwana kicked and sliced.

Morwenna Rowe whacked and whacked again, then stabbed a hole right through it.

Daphne stamped and smashed.

The demon was a mess, squealing on the floor, shrinking. And then it started crying.

'Oh, finish it off, dear,' said Morwenna Rowe. 'It's starting to look pathetic.'

Daphne picked up the shrinking, powerless demon, and threw it into the stream where it landed with a small splash. 'Dead in the river, you fuck.' With her anger rising, she raised the bar, and an end started to glow red, and grew brighter. Daphne felt the heat radiating onto her face. 'You killed my mum. You killed Mrs Legge. You did this. You did all of this. Die, you fucker, die!'

She stabbed the red spike through its head, and it screeched a final screech, thrashed and flailed, and disappeared as though dissolving into the water. And then it was gone.

Daphne looked up at Morwenna and Gugwana. They looked surprisingly lively for mannequins, and surprisingly plastic for those who could move like that. Still, Daphne didn't give it more than a passing thought. 'Where's Alfie?' she asked.

'With his mother,' said Gugwana.

'Sara's okay?'

'She will be. Deanna is keeping them safe. The demons are all gone now.'

'Not yet,' said Daphne. 'There are more.'

'Oh?' said Gugwana.

'There's a whole load of them. In my basement. I accidentally let one out. It's the biggest I've seen.'

Morwenna Rowe and Gugwana looked at each other.

Gugwana smiled. 'If you let it out, it is yours to deal with. And if you let it out, it means you are ready. But right now, if a demon remains loose, we will get back to the house and protect the basement door, and the child. You will be just fine, my dear.'

Morwenna Rowe looked at Gugwana. 'We should warn her.'

That got Daphne's attention.

Gugwana looked straight at Daphne. 'Daphne, my dear friend and sister. It may be big, but it is not powerful, weakened by all of the years held in the dark. It will fall more easily than you might think. But it has other tricks.

Mind tricks. This is what you must endure. But, as always, be strong, and you will win.'

'They have been using mind tricks all along.'

'Of course, dear, that's all they do. It's what they were created for. But this one is different. It has tricks that will be new to you despite being those that you have dealt with all along.'

'I don't need more riddles now. I need to know what it's going to do.'

'The same mind tricks,' Morwenna Rowe said, 'that it has been doing since you were a child. And though they were dimmed while it was trapped deep down in the darkness, now it is up in the light, you will see them in full brightness. Do not delay us further, we must protect the house.' The two plastic witches stiffly made their way down the path back through the woodland towards Hanging Hill Lane. Daphne wanted to stop them, to get more information. But she knew she couldn't keep them with her. There was a special house that needed their protection, and there was a child inside. She let them go, and was, again, alone.

Daphne held the bar over her shoulder and continued to walk along the stream, leaving the sisters behind her.

She passed a few more things she recognised as she continued her hunt. A small piece of paper – a card with the number for the police who had been to visit her, PCs Bach and Trevithick. A pile of wet, broken tea bags. Her television, smashed to pieces.

She was distracted when she saw a photograph lying on some damp leaves. The image was of her, looking at the camera, two red eyes behind her by her stairs. The distraction didn't last long. Seconds later, a sobbing.

Through the leaves, there he was.

Charl.

Another from her list.

Chapter Thirty-seven

CHARL LAY ON HIS back, head against a tree twisted in a position that looked more than a little painful, crying, an utterly terrified look on his face, veins bulging around bloodshot eyes, his arms quivering.

Daphne checked her surroundings. She wasn't going to fall into a trap now. She kept her guard up as she approached.

Charl saw Daphne and appeared to try to bury himself in the soil around him. The distress he was showing was incredible, and unless Charl was a superb actor, and he might well have been, this looked very real. Daphne checked around her again, and all seemed calm and still. When she looked back at Charl, she saw it. A small glass container next to him. She picked it up, then looked around again, making sure she wasn't about to spring a trap. Still, no one. Nothing.

When she read the label on the small jar, all became clear. *Devil's Fungus*. She knew exactly what had happened. She knew about that one now. Extreme mental distress ending almost always in suicide. Cured only by seven grains of love salt and – although she assumed the second part was a joke on the part of her mother – a kick up the backside.

Daphne watched Charl writhe on the floor. In any other circumstances, such anguish would have been horrifying to see. On Charl, it was kind of satisfying. Daphne reached into her pocket and pulled out the love salt jar. She figured she could pick out at least six grains before refocusing on Charl, the piskie trickster, the one who had played her friend and gained her trust only to betray her in a way that had Alfie taken by a demon and Sara's head crushed. He lay quivering in anguish on the floor, now trying to tunnel through the bark of a large old tree, his fingers raw, and bloody bone sticking out where his fingertips used to be.

Daphne pushed her fingertip into the jar and rubbed it on the glass as she withdrew it. She looked closely at her finger. It was hard to see exactly how many, but there were a few tiny sparkles there. Around six, maybe seven. It would probably do the job. She crouched down next to Charl's head, whose tears intensified as he looked up at her, both terrified of her and as though he was pleading for forgiveness.

'Help,' he cried softly.

Daphne looked at the grains on her finger. Then at Charl. Then she smiled. 'Okay, Charl, it'll be okay.' She then put her finger into her own mouth, tasted the salty flavour, and pulled her finger back out. 'Seems like I'll forgive myself for this one.' She smiled.

Charl turned over and started to dig through the hard roots, though he didn't make any progress at all. He picked up a large rock, stopped, looked at it and screamed, and buried his head in his arms. Then got back to digging some more.

Daphne smiled as she walked back to the stream, closer to the bean-nighe's bridge, leaving Charl's squealing and despairing screams floating through the trees and bushes behind her.

Chapter Thirty-eight

THE BEAN-NIGHE. THE TRICKSTER.

Her head would look good face down in the shallow water under the bridge, her fat shoulders motionless and bloodying the wet mud, the clothes on fire all around her. This old hag had caused such pain, such suffering, and was so revolting in every way imaginable. Daphne would enjoy this one a lot.

The hag crouched over the stream, dipping some fabric, wheezing as she sang a song that somehow managed to sound as ugly and disgusting as she looked. On the floor, a piece of paper waved in the wind. Daphne picked the page up. The words at the top: *Daphne's epilogue*. The completion of the poem that Daphne had started to read in her mother's scrapbook. Her mother had really finished it. Emotion washed through Daphne at the thought she would get to read it. A mix of relief, love and pain. But now was not the time to be taken off her guard.

Laughter took Daphne's attention. Something in the leaves above. A familiar laughter that had haunted her since she was a child. And a huge *wooshhhhh* slid through the trees and burning embers floated by in the breeze.

Daphne folded the paper, pushed it into her pocket, and gripped the thin metal bar tight as she approached the source of the sound. In the clearing behind the bushes stood the giant demon. She had only seen it once before, as it had left her basement and run through her lounge, laughing as it went, and yet it seemed deeply familiar. The giant stood, towering high, looking straight at her, laughing in a way that wiped all the emotion in Daphne immediately away. Although she had only seen it once before, she knew that demon face. And although she had only heard it once before, she knew that demon laugh. Both had taunted her before. A very long time ago.

That face had been the very face of the demon mask on the boy on the Halloween Hell Float, Marcus the bully boy, all those years ago. The cutting laugh was his, Marcus's horrible, mean laugh. It was like that demon had been in that boy, stalking her since she was a child. Perhaps it had always been close to her, always within striking distance, always pushing its influence on her. It was in her basement and perhaps always had been.

Now she was going to kill it.

Daphne stepped into the clearing, gripping her iron bar. Her anger rose, and one end of the metal started to glow hot and red. She knew how to do this. Straight into the eyehole, just as Agatha Hunter had told her. Immediately and with no hesitation. She walked up to the huge demon, which just laughed at her before its face settled on a mocking grin. She had the knowledge to beat it. She had the belief. She had the weapon. If only she had the height to reach its eyes. The demon laughed as though it knew. Always looking down on her. Forever-mocking.

'What's up, shorty?' the giant hissed, and laughed again. It was a horrible, biting laugh, but Daphne wouldn't let it hurt.

Daphne took a swing at the huge creature. The iron spike bounced off its armoured skin, and as it did, the beast seemed to grow taller.

'This is over. I've beaten you all. You're the last one.'

'All of us?' replied the demon. What about them over there?'

Nearby stood a group of her old school friends, still children, laughing at her. She looked back at the demon, who now stood in light so bright she had to shield her painful eyes. The light came from the Halloween Hell Float, chugging through the trees, its carnival lights flashing and shining, and there the demon stood, and as her vision returned, on the back of the vehicle looking just like the boy, Marcus, that had laughed at her that horrible day Daphne had last worn her majorette's uniform. Anger rose inside her and she raised her metal bar. But when she looked at it, it was no longer a metal bar. Everything was different. Now she held just a majorette's baton; her hand was that of a child's. The demon laughed at her, and gestured to her friends to laugh too. And they did. Each laugh cut through separately, chiding, mocking, piercing. Daphne found her whole body shrinking. She was just a child holding a baton, facing a giant demon, blinded by lights, taunted from all directions.

'Stop!' she shouted and a familiar desire washed over her. She wanted to become invisible. A little, safe, nobody. Her voice sounded like a child's.

'Invisible like this?' asked the demon, perhaps reading her mind, and as it faded from view, the lights dimmed and the whole Halloween Hell Float fell to darkness and the demon disappeared with it. Behind it shone a bright full moon, and everything went quiet.

Two piskies stumbled in front of her, walking across the clearing. She raised her baton to protect herself, but then realised that she was not in danger. The looks on their faces betrayed love, and the thieves of the love salts were revealed. Daphne didn't care. She was too busy feeling tiny, herself the size of a piskie, hoping that no one would notice her and wishing she could just go home.

Laughter, all around again. Music sounded in the distance, getting closer, distorted, heavy guitars, deep drums, and the Hell Float appeared, chugging through the woodland with its steaming chimneys billowing steam and smoke, cinders raining all around, bright lights and what looked like giant, real bones pushing the wheels around. Children dressed as demons stood around the huge machine laughing at her, laughing at stupid Daphne, the huge demon from the back pointing, laughing, mocking as music blared and the singer from the band walked to the edge of the float and took his position by a microphone. The Hell Float moved across the woods, tall and long, obscuring the full moon, an army of kids on the side, firing out jets of smoke and steam around it, kids, so many kids alongside and on top, demon masks on, pointing at her, laughing.

The band atop the Hell Float started to sing. The band were grown men, muscular, dressed in black leather and masks, the guitar tones heavy and thick, the drumming solid and tight. 'YOU'LL GO DOWN, DOWN, DOWN TO THE UNDERGROUND, WHERE THE DEAD REACH UP AND THEY'LL PULL YOU DOWN,' they sang in dark, full tones, 'DOWN THAT DEEP AND WIDE AND LONELY DEEP DARK HOLE.'

Daphne felt her strength drain away.

Still, she swung her baton up at the demon on the float, but she was too short, she couldn't even reach its armoured shins.

Cracking sounds from her left. She swung her head around, and the earth below the leaves moved.

Cracking sounds from her right, and the earth was moving. A hand pushed through the soil, then another. And another. Dirty human hands.

'DOWN, DOWN, DOWN TO THE UNDERGROUND...' the band sang.

More human hands and arms pushed through, dirty and rotting, the skin peeling off, and Daphne turned to run from the sight, from the smell, but the majorette troop were behind her, twirling batons high, marching on the spot, laughing at her and ready to swing at her if she tried to move past them.

She swung back around, and the Hell Float chugged through the trees again, lights blinding her, and the rotting people pulled themselves slowly from the soil into the thick smoky air.

Rotting humans. Dead humans. Familiar humans.

'...WHERE THE DEAD RISE UP AND THEY'LL PULL YOU DOWN...' sang the band atop the float, the drums pounding as hard and tight as the muscles on the guitarist's huge arms, flames shooting up behind them into the night sky.

To the right, the first dead person out of the ground stepped into the light. A policeman, one who had knocked on the door during the killings on her street, then another, another dead policeman hauled itself from the mud and fallen leaves. Another followed, a giant of a man, the huge policeman she had met two years ago, emerged from the mud, rotting, dead, the throat slit.

The huge demon appeared in front of her eyes, flames pouring from its nostrils, and Daphne swung her baton at it with all the power she could muster, driven by fear, driven by anger, but the demon just laughed and grew bigger and Daphne felt heat from it like from a raging fire.

The band played on, chugging guitars, low-pitched, growling voices, 'DOWN THAT DEEP AND DARK AND LONELY DEEP DARK HOLE GOING DOWN, DOWN, DOWN TO THE UNDERGROUND...'

To the left, more dead. The three killed at the beach murders. Boddy. Head. Brendan Burger. Three men in boat crew uniforms staggered from beneath the surface, heads in pieces, brains showing.

'...WHERE THE DEAD RISE UP AND THEY'LL PULL YOU DOWN...' came through the trees, louder, louder.

A headless man followed from the ground, turned, and reached into the soil, pulling out his head. Another police uniform. The policeman held his head high above his shoulders, and Daphne recognised the pale, terrified-looking face. She couldn't remember a full name. All she could remember was *Casper*.

All people that had died because of her. All people killed by the demons to get to Daphne. All the poor humans who had done nothing wrong but had died because of her. Mrs Legge's torso wriggled from the ground, and Daphne was again reminded of her mother, and, weirdly, in amongst the horror and feelings of helplessness, felt a glimmer of hope.

'...DOWN THAT DEEP AND WIDE AND LONELY DEEP DARK HOLE GOING DOWN, DOWN, DOWN...'

The demon, that giant demon laughed at her as the Hell Float chugged by, band playing loud, drums pounding, smoke spewing in jets, the truck sending her jumping out of the way, and Daphne swung her baton at the demon, but she was too small, and she missed, and as the Hell Float passed her it revealed behind it giant spiders, dancing in time to the music that blared. Daphne swung around to run, but still there they were, the majorettes, marching on the spot, twirling, clowns behind them laughing at her like maniacs, dancing carnival beasts moving through the woodland on her flanks, Mrs Legge face down in pieces in the stream next to her.

Daphne swung around again, disorientated by the smoke and trees and the sheer volume of the pounding band. As the Hell Float chugged past again through the trees, steam gushing from the chimney, lights blinding and music blaring, the moon beyond, the demon swung out a huge tree branch it held in its claws, connecting hard to Daphne's head.

She fell.

The last thing she felt before her consciousness gave way was the cold water on her face and all through her body. The last thing she heard was the splash of water, then a world that quickly became muffled and quiet. As she drew a breath, water entered her mouth and her lungs, and as she lay face down in the stream, the sound of the band now dull and distant, everything turned to shadowy grey and the shadows swirled and thickened and turned to black, and the world turned to black with them.

* * * * *

Daphne felt herself sinking, the sound from all around dulling. Though the stream was but a few inches deep, she felt the water engulf her and the mud in her face give way, and with it, darkness below opened up and spread all around as she sank deeper, deeper down through the dark and dirty water that swallowed her.

And though she felt an urge to fight it, to float, to breathe and live, the urge was pulled out of her by the long fingers that reached up from below, grabbing her ankles and pinching her wrists, gripping and stroking her neck softly, bony fingers squeezing and pulling on her toes, so many hands, all grabbing and dragging her down, then the faces came. Faces of her old neighbours, one by one, of Luke from number six, Luke the gentle first boy she had ever dated, and his parents who had also been bloodily murdered by the demons, the faces swam and swirled in front of her and more hands kept coming, peeling hands of the five who lived at ten, hands of all the Hanging Hill Lane dead that gripped her and pulled her down through the murky water, ghostly apparitions of the four who lived at eight, their faces floating in front of Daphne's as she sank like an anchor, eight more slippery hands rising up from the depths and dragging her down by the wrists and ankles, down, all the way down, pulling, pulling until the last of Daphne's breath had snuck from her and just an ounce of fight remained. Looking hopelessly down into the murky depths, there they were, demons, demons all the way down, pulling on the ankles of the Hanging Hill dead, the dead with their skeletal hands on Daphne, their decaying arms around her, dragging her down, that final ounce of fight disappearing in the face of the demons in the deep, before the hands slid from her body and left her to float limply, left her all alone in the darkness and black as her breathing stopped and her body felt so cold and useless and light.

Chapter Thirty-nine

SPLASH!

Again. Another.

The world, full of nothing but dim, grim water. Another *splash* – a shape from nearby – an ant from above, clasping its throat, drowning in the water moving through the darkness and watery shadows.

More ants. More giant splashes; ants all around and above her, some gasping for breath, some fighting for their lives, some lying lifeless in the water rising up and up.

A hand on the shoulder, fingers digging in, shaking her.

'Leave me alone. You've won. I'm dying.'

Small hands. Behind, submerged in the deep, a blurry view of more ants falling from the giant dome in the sky, splashing all around and sinking past her.

'No.' The voice of a young girl. 'Fight.' The majorette, painfully worried alongside her in the water.

'I can't. There's too many. They're too strong. If I die here they can't take me. I'm sorry. I'm really so sorry.'

'No!' a familiar voice, loud, so loud, and a blurry image of Daphne's mother's face shimmering through the water above her, breaking the surface, getting closer.

'It's games.' A twirl of the child's stick. 'It moves smoothly through the water as if in air. See?'

'Mind games, I know,' said Daphne weakly. 'But they're too strong.'

'Games in whose mind, dear daughter?'

More giant ants cascaded from above and crashed and struggled in the water.

Daphne hesitated, embraced the peace, and replied, 'Mine. My mind.'

'And if the games are all in your mind, then who makes the rules?'

Daphne thought for a few seconds, fighting the wonderful feeling of relaxation creeping in to take her. 'I do. I make the rules.'

'So how can they beat you, when you make the rules?'

Daphne almost felt herself smile.

'They cannot control your thoughts, your feelings, your magic. You control that. Try.'

Confidence rose up, pushing out the water which drained away. The ants who looked drowned now breathed again.

'You're doing that,' said the majorette as the water swirled and gushed into the darkness.

'Your mind, your world, your rules,' said her mother with a smile.

'Mine too,' said the majorette.

The water level dropped fast. A soggy, bedraggled ant walked over to Daphne and looked her straight in the eye.

'Who are you?' asked Daphne.

'We are parts of you,' said the ant. 'Now, there is only one of that demon, and there are thousands of us. It needn't be a fair fight.' The ant grinned. The grin looked like her own. It had the family magic in it.

'Listen to him,' said Daphne's mother with a wonderful smile. 'But right now, you need to roll over.'

'Roll over.' It was the majorette, young Daphne.

'Roll over.' It was the ant.

'Roll over.' It was a larger ant as it approached.

'Roll over.' It was a distant ant in the dome.

'Roll over.' It was a purple-blue Paulie-bird as it turned to a green glow, smiling, and Daphne wanted to pluck it from the sky and squeeze it in her arms.

She nodded, and rolled over, and gasped.

When she opened her eyes, the Hell Float had passed and the chimney steam was clearing, the moon behind no longer there.

Chapter Forty

IN PLACE OF THE moon shone five bright stars.

I'll always be inside here, said the voice of her mother from inside. *I live here now, remember.* Daphne shot a look at Mrs Legge, moving slug-slow towards her like a wounded earthworm. Another corpse pushed from the ground. A man in a shirt wearing rubber gloves, a fish hook dangling from each eye.

'...TO THE UNDERGROUND WHERE THE DEAD RISE UP AND THEY'LL PULL YOU DOWN...' Tom-toms pounded tightly and a bass drum thudded, cymbals crashed and a fuzzy bass growled.

I can beat it, came the voice of young Daphne from deep inside her mind.

Daphne felt her strength rise. *Mind games.* She stepped forward between the walking corpses, towards the demon on the Halloween Hell Float, whose laugh grew louder, more mocking. Through the trees, the other carnival floats arrived, blaring a cacophony of music and engines and laughter.

And the carnival caravans grew closer.

And the ghosts of her past did all laugh.

The crowds, they pointed and snickered and chose her.

And the ghosts of her past did all laugh.

'...Down that deep and wide and lonely deep dark hole...'

Daphne felt herself grow taller as she took in the light from the five shining stars. She stepped closer, closer to the Hell Float, and the demon roared with chiding laughter, pointing at her, laughing with her old school friends by the trees, the whole carnival crowds made up of the Hanging Hill Lane dead, who pointed and laughed with them.

Trust me, I can beat it now, said the voice of the child within.

Your mind, your world, your rules, came the voice of her mother.

She stepped closer still, looking up at the huge demon, the five stars shining bright above the giant's head, and with every step she took, the demon seemed to shrink. 'You can't beat us,' she said, moving closer and closer, feeling the baton in her hand, her fingers beginning to twitch with muscle memory from a long time ago.

The demon remained unflinching, laughter bellowing louder, but still shrinking with every step she took.

'There are a hundred who stand and laugh at you.'

'And there are a thousand ants looking back. You cannot see them, but they are real. These people are not.'

Daphne was just a few feet away now, and the demon's laughter grew louder, and Daphne saw that it had nothing, no form of attack or defence, nothing, nothing but mocking laughter and mind games, and she took another step and the demon shrunk further and the baton started to twist between her fingers, and she raised it higher as another carnival float steamed by, mechanical laughter blaring from speakers behind theatrical smoke that smelled of death.

'...DOWN, DOWN, DOWN TO THE UNDERGROUND...'

'My world,' Daphne said as she marched towards the demon, 'my rules.'

She was sure she saw the demon flinch, but then its laugh got louder, more pointed, meaner, and the face of the young boy underneath it showed through, somehow bringing pain to Daphne's gut. It was like she could see the sadness in the face of the child that it sought to mask with its bullying laughter, poor, scared little Marcus. Scared Marcus: another mask worn by the demon in an attempt to beat her, and she felt the laughter bounce off her as though she wore armour that protected her from it.

I don't care about him anymore, said the voice of the child from within.

The band's drums fell out of time, the vocals thinner and higher in pitch, missing beats, singing sharp then flat.

Daphne felt herself giggle, and she saw the fear in the demon boy's eyes. 'You know what Agatha Hunter told me, how to kill you?' she said to the demon.

'What?' it mumbled through fake laughter.

'She said for me to stick this up your arsehole.' Daphne sniggered, and the demon stopped its taunting immediately. Horror crept over its face as Daphne twirled the majorette baton high and fast, spinning with such speed the ends were imperceptible – until one end started to glow red. 'I don't care anymore!' she bellowed, feeling her adult voice return to her and she felt something shift in the air around her as she began to grow once more. 'It doesn't matter anymore. I don't care!'

'She dropped it because she was stupid!' bellowed the demon back.

'No. She was not. I have a lot of fucks to give, but none are for you,' Daphne said, before she caught her breath and sang quietly, 'I don't care.' And then on a whispered breath, 'My world, my rules, fuckhead. And I just don't care.'

They were the words on which the children turned.

The children all began to run, some disappeared into nothingness before they could take more than three steps, and the mocking sounds stopped dead. The Halloween Hell Float sank down and shrank as its tyres hissed and deflated, and pieces of Halloween Hell scenery, the giant bones and steaming chimneys started to fall off. Other children dressed as demons ran into the woods, some disappeared into thin air, one shouted, 'It wasn't me,' before crying and crouching into a ball and exploding into dust. The band played on briefly, just children, playing out-of-time tinny drums and out-of-tune guitars. The laughing crowds fell silent and dispersed. One by one, the dead people fell to their knees, the skin rotted completely off, their flesh fell to the ground, just slabs of rotting meat with flies buzzing around, and their skeletons shattered and landed on the woodland floor, leaves blowing up and around to conceal where they fell as the meat rotted and disappeared in front of her eyes. The band disappeared, leaving an electric guitar lying on the top of the float, feedback ringing. More pieces of carnival machinery fell in a heap in the steam and smoke as the Halloween Hell Float crumbled around the once-huge demon and Daphne stepped up and stopped the baton spinning in her hand.

Behind her, a troupe of majorettes looked innocent and pretty as they smiled and danced in their uniforms, marching on the spot in perfect time, twirling their batons in unison, looking to Daphne for guidance. She'd missed that memory. Those other girls had really looked up to her.

Daphne turned to the demon and said through her teeth, 'I do not care about you anymore.'

She did not dally.

She held up her iron bar – no longer a child's baton – in one hand, and thrust it hard towards the demon's eye.

An inch before impact, the demon grabbed the end, and gripped it hard in its claws. Daphne pushed with all her strength towards the eye. The demon pushed back.

Daphne screamed, 'My world, my rules.'

The demon pushed back harder, forcing the iron bar from its eye. 'But you are weak, so small.'

'My world. My rules!'

'Tiny, insubstantial little girl, weak like a worm.'

'My world. My rules!' she shouted, and the back spike of the bar burst into flames. Fear flashed on the demon's face, the weapon still an inch from its eye.

'You cannot do this. You are a tiny little stupid girl, useless.'

'My world, my rules!' she shouted back, and the front spike of the bar engulfed itself in flames, blistering the demon's hand.

'No!' shouted the demon, releasing the iron bar and smashing Daphne back with its other hand.

Daphne found her balance a few paces back, holding up the spiked bar, aflame at both ends. She stepped forward, and muscle memory from a long, long time ago moved the thin cylindrical iron bar, a rotation, another, another, faster, spinning around as she moved forwards, the fiery iron bar always steady and safe. When she grabbed it firmly and the spinning stopped, a flaming spike pointed directly at the demon's face. And Daphne was no longer a child.

She plunged the burning iron spike into the demon's head which hissed and popped and crackled and the rest of the Hell Float crumpled as if made of card and paper, and caught fire and turned to smoke and blew softly into the sky, wafted up by the wind, obscuring the five shining stars. The demon screeched and gasped, its pitch matching the feedback of the guitars, and the sound became one as it faded away. The body of the beast flailed in the light of the flaming float, and then it was gone. It was all gone.

It was all quiet.

It was all still.

Daphne checked her surroundings and saw that all was safe, open space where the majorettes had been, and she looked to the sky. As the last of the Hell Float steam and smoke dissipated, it revealed behind it the full moon, shining bright.

A duck flew past the glowing moon.

And all felt good and lighter and right.

Daphne took a deep breath and turned around, metal bar in her hand, the glow on the end subsiding. She had won.

It was time to go home.

The peaceful feeling of finality didn't last long. She saw it. The one thing that could stop this from being quite over.

Staring at her through the trees was the ugliest creature she had ever seen.

The bean-nighe hocked a globule of phlegm the size of an egg and dribbled it from her lower lip onto the earth between her feet.

The bean-nighe. The washerwoman. The hag.

The last one on the list.

Chapter Forty-one

IT WAS A STRANGE feeling.

The bean-nighe had caused so much pain, and she had been so mocking as she had done it. She was a despicable piece of evil, the most deserving of revenge. Yet, now, with the demons removed from Daphne's world, the desire to kill her seemed to have gone. No longer did Daphne want to ram that metal rod through her skull. She was an old woman, pretty defenceless without the demons or the piskies, and bashing her head in on the dirt seemed somehow a little unfair now.

Daphne took the list from her pocket, and the pen, and looked down at the paper, then back up at the bean-nighe, who stood there, worry on her face. Daphne crossed out the names which she had destroyed. The head piskie. Two

261

demons. Her pen hovered over the name Charl, then she crossed it out. All that remained was the bean-nighe. She pushed the paper and pen back into her pocket and looked up at the ugly old washerwoman.

'Sorry,' Daphne said. 'You're on the list.'

The bean-nighe turned and ran, but she was so heavy and immobile that Daphne caught her in seconds, grabbing her by the fabric on the back of her stinking coat, and wrestled her away down the path towards Hanging Hill Lane.

Through the woods one stalked and one waddled, past the rubbish that lay all through the woodland. Daphne's mother's good crockery set, now smashed into pieces lying by a rock on the path. More old textbooks. The large cooking pot that Daphne had put bugs and beetles in as a child. It was all there, in front of her, yet gone from her life now.

As she prodded the bean-nighe's huge body down the path, she saw another familiar sight. A tree with hard roots above the earth, and lying on them, covered in blood, Charl.

Charl lay still and lifeless. His tiny hands lay either side of the large rock almost like they were gripping it still, his head batted and skull crushed next to it, blood and brains pooling.

Daphne gripped her iron bar and without warning or hesitation, smashed the spike into the bean-nighe's knee, who crumpled to the floor, wailing in pain.

Charl's body lay still, his head in pieces, his finger bones worn down to the knuckles. And although he was dead and gone, Daphne still felt her anger rise again. As it did, a spike of her metal bar glowed red hot. She pushed it into Charl's robe and blew, setting the fabric alight, and within seconds, Charl's small body was ablaze. 'Told you you'd burn,' she stated flatly.

As Daphne stepped back, she got a nose full of smoke, a nose full of burning meat. It smelled good. Reminiscent of piskie pie.

The bean-nighe finally shut up, her cries of pain subsiding. Of the whole list, only the bean-nighe remained, and her demise would be imminent, the disgusting old hag.

Daphne wrestled her through the woods, the smoking piskie body behind her, the smell getting fainter with every step. The washerwoman gave up struggling as they passed the toppled stack of stones and stepped on to the bottom of Hanging Hill Lane, where Daphne pushed her out from the trees. She dragged her up the path of number two and in through the vacant doorway, through the hallway, and threw the bean-nighe into the lounge.

'What are you going to do with me?' grunted the hag.

'A question for a question,' replied Daphne, putting her hand in her pocket.

The hag stared back, dribble dropping onto the carpet from her disgusting mouth. Eventually she spoke. 'Very well. What is your question?'

'I'll think of one,' said Daphne. 'You did it. You killed Sara. You had Alfie infested. And, by the way, he'll be just fine. You lost. You all lost. I won.'

'You cannot kill me, witch,' said the bean-nighe. 'For I am already long dead.'

'I know,' said Daphne. 'But that doesn't mean we can't say goodbye forever.' Daphne grabbed the carpet from the corner of the room and tugged hard, revealing the hatch. She knelt, pulled the key from her pocket, and took the padlock in her fingers.

Click.

The bean-nighe tried to run for the door, but she was so ungainly, so fat and clumsy, that she had barely made three steps before Daphne simply walked over and grabbed her by some useful rolls of back fat.

Daphne almost smiled. 'Where are you going, bean-bitch?' she said as the washerwoman fought weakly and Daphne yanked her across the room to the hatch and tripped her. She fell hard onto the floorboards near to where the knobble had been.

Daphne pulled on the handle, and screeches came from deep below. Roars followed, getting closer from the depths.

'Goodbye,' said Daphne, as she bounced the bean-nighe across the floorboards, and struggle as she might, the hag couldn't stop Daphne from pushing her head and shoulders into the hole. The bean-nighe clung on to the edge, but Daphne gave her one last good, hard shove, and the bean-nighe fell with a long, fading scream. Daphne slammed the hatch shut quickly and snapped the padlock back into place.

She was gone.

They were all gone.

Daphne rolled the carpet back over the hatch. She took off one shoe and pressed her foot against the bump. As she did, for the first time in a long time, her tears felt good. As did the knobble.

And then the sirens came and blue lights flashed through the window, and vehicles rolled down the road outside.

Chapter Forty-two

THE HATCH WAS CLOSED, locked and hidden. Whatever was down there could stay there for a very long time for all Daphne cared.

She looked through the curtainless window. Fire engines, three of them, blue lights spiralling, men and women jumping out and running into the woods. Daphne stepped outside and walked up her path.

'What's going on?' she asked.

A fireman stopped. 'Fire in the woods. Just go inside, please.'

Daphne smirked. 'Must be the fire ants.'

'Not funny.' The man shot back an unimpressed look as Daphne turned and walked back into her house with a grin.

She made her way up the stairs, the second one creaked, sounding somehow soft and comforting.

She poked her head around her bedroom door. Everything was as she had left it, aside from the pointed broomstick, which Morwenna Rowe had been in to claim. It was hers anyway.

Alfie flinched as she entered her mother's room, and Daphne knew to be calm and soft. Gugwana sat on the bed. She looked less plastic every time Daphne saw her. Morwenna Rowe stood looking out the window, monitoring the outside. She didn't turn her head. Deanna Tamblyn walked stiffly towards her, raised a plastic hand, and put it on Daphne's cheek. Alfie stood, vacantly staring, holding Gugwana's plastic hand.

'The world feels different, does it not?' said Deanna.

It did. It felt lighter. 'Thank you, Deanna. But please excuse me, I have work to do.'

Daphne walked over to the mannequin in her mother's clothes, just shiny and unreal and lifeless, and after stroking the cold cheek one last time, removed the clothing.

With each beautiful garment she pulled from the plastic and dropped onto the floor, hope fell too, until the dummy was naked. The pile of fabric looked so familiar, yet useless, so pointless on the dusty floor. When she bent down to pick them up, her stomach cramped and she struggled to stand. She hugged them close and gripped them in her fingers and squeezed her eyes so hard that the world stood still and empty. When her breathing finally softened, the physical pain subsided as she stood, and she tried desperately to block out the reality of what she was doing as she gently folded the clothes on the bed, as if watching her arms move from another pair of eyes that weren't so close. She placed the clothes neatly in a pile in the back of the wardrobe and closed the mirrored door, revealing her own face to her.

It looked dirty. It was cut. It looked tired. But mostly, it looked peaceful.

Daphne picked up the pile of the clothes that Agatha Hunter had been swept away in, and re-dressed the mannequin. This time, she watched her hands work through eyes that felt like her own.

'You're getting quite the collection of witches,' Gugwana said quietly with a friendly smile. 'You've done well to keep us going.'

'Will you keep improving? Will you all be normal again?'

'Oh my dear, we were never normal. We will be functional again.'

'Sara?' Daphne asked.

'She, we, you. All of us, except, well, I'm sorry,' said Gugwana.

Mum wasn't there anymore. Not even in plastic form. Daphne's amazing mother was gone.

Morwenna Rowe turned from the window. Her face looked almost human. 'There is no sign of the demons. You have done well.'

'They are still here. In the basement. Lots of them, I don't know how many.'

'Oh my dear,' said Gugwana. 'They will always go all the way down. Beat one, and there will always be another. Sometimes it's best to just hide them away. Beat the real troublemakers if you like or need, but sometimes you can just bury the rest and get on with your life.'

'So they're okay down there? They won't come out?'

'If you're okay with them down there, then the rest of the world won't care.'

'It'll be okay?'

'Oh Daphne,' Deanna Tamblyn said, some sternness returning, 'when will you just learn to do what you want?'

Morwenna Rowe picked up her broomstick and put the ornate metal cover over the spike. 'Looks like I'll be getting home then. There will be much dusting and cobwebbing to do. And I must first nip into the woods and disappear the chip shop lady before they find her. Your possessions are littered through the woodland and there is a cut up corpse amongst them. In the future, you must think of these things. But for now, well done.'

'Thank you, Morwenna,' said Daphne.

Gugwana stood, gently passing Alfie's hand to Deanna. Gugwana hugged Daphne and the two old, rubbery witches left without a sound beyond a creak.

'I'll stay here,' said Deanna Tamblyn. 'I'll bring these two on and watch the child. You go on. Do what you want to do. What you really want to do. You don't have to worry about the demons anymore.'

That's when the love salt kicked in, and Daphne put on some music, and danced.

* * * * *

Three days later, Alfie returned to his old, cheeky self, his dimples were back in his cheeks and he was laughing at every face Daphne pulled, even when he was so tired he was ready to sleep. The police came around a couple of times looking for Sara, but Daphne assured them that she was fine and she'd just nipped out. They never returned.

That morning, returning from the shops, Daphne stopped dead at the end of her garden path, her heart in her mouth. Three piskies stood in her doorway. Two held on to her front door, the other held a hammer. Two more scampered out from the house. They all looked terrified the moment they saw her.

'Worry not,' said Morwenna Rowe, startling Daphne from her garden across the street. 'They're just doing a little job for me, no need to bake a piskie pie.' They parted and let Daphne back into her house, which felt different now. Lighter. With somehow more air. Warmer. Inside was a pile of Daphne's things, returned from the woodland, and two more sheepish-looking piskies putting them back where they'd come from. Daphne unboxed her new phone, and no sooner than she had installed her messenger app, a new message from Olivia popped up. Sorry I went AWOL, had some thinking to do. Ever have any more demon trouble, I'll be right over! We'll kill 'em! Beach this weekend? she wrote. Daphne couldn't help but laugh.

A week later, news broke in the local community of another missing person, Cathy Legge from the local fish and chip shop. By the following week, the news story had ended, fizzled out and faded away.

Three months later, the mannequins wearing the clothes of Sara and her mother were starting to resemble them, and Deanna Tamblyn dropped in daily, carrying a tray of tea into the room.

Daphne too felt happier. Lighter. Warmer. The voice of her mother that called from within would never be good enough, but now she knew that she was what kept that part of her in the world, and that would have to be enough.

It would never be enough, but that would have to be as close to okay as she could accept. She would make the rest up as she went along.

One day, when Daphne visited the mannequins, Deanna Tamblyn put her hand on her shoulder.

'Of all our teachings, my dear Daphne, you have not done the most important one. Still, you dally.'

'What's that? What did I miss?'

'Do you want to stay in this empty home with nothing but memories, alone, aside from a couple of old witches passing through? Or do you want to do something else? Go and see those gold sand beaches with the palm trees? Like you said to the coin.'

'How did you know that?'

'I have ears, Daphne. Now, please, go and do what you want to do.'

'Just walk off into the sunset, like a cliché?'

Deanna Tamblyn shook her head and smiled. 'Your world, your rules, sister.'

The first thing Daphne did after Deanna Tamblyn left was call Paulie. They worked things out in no time. The second thing she did was book a flight to the tropics. One way. With Paulie. Lovely, kind, gentle, forgiving Paulie. She would return when she was ready. If they wanted to.

Chapter Forty-three

DAPHNE STOOD ON HER doorstep with her backpack strapped on. The bag weighed her down, but in other ways, she still felt somehow lighter than she had done a few weeks before.

Gugwana stood with her, her clothes and smile lighting up the lane as they had done for as long as Daphne could remember.

And then a feeling hit her that used to be all too familiar. Fear. It came out of nowhere and filled her gut, and for a second, she thought she was going to throw up. Gugwana took her hand, smiling softly and knowingly.

'Why am I so scared of going?' Daphne asked. 'If I'm so brave, why am I so scared of this? I'm shitting myself.'

'If you weren't scared of it, then doing it wouldn't be brave, would it now?'

Daphne felt her hands shake and her knees start to weaken. After all she'd been through, how could the simple act of getting in a taxi bring her to the edge of panic? But she was going for a reason. A good one.

'You want me to walk with you to the top?'

'No, thank you. You go in and get the kettle on.' Daphne didn't want company. She wanted to walk off and panic in peace, as best as her shaky legs would take her up the hill, alone, and she knew very well she might cry. Anyway, she liked being alone, and there was nothing wrong with that.

Gugwana hinted at the offer of a hug, and Daphne squeezed her hard. As she turned, she saw Morwenna Rowe waving from the other side of the glass in the house opposite. Daphne smiled and waved back.

As she walked up the hill past Sara's house, then number six, eight and ten, the boards on the windows now showing some age, she felt something stir and grip in the pit of her stomach. It felt like loss, but deeper, both familiar and different. It was grief of a new kind. Grief and longing for her childhood that had as much chance of coming back as her mother, yet would always remain with her as a faint whisper and in her memories, to come back to haunt and warm her dreams.

The demons had taken the dying days of her childhood. The piskies had taken the rest. But time would have taken it anyway.

As one foot stepped in front of the other, she knew she couldn't turn back. If she returned to number two now because of her strengthening painful but temporary emotions, her own demons would feed and feast on them and become stronger. There was nothing left for her at number two but demons all the way down. She had to push on. And so she did, under the leafy trees and past the corner which she would always remember as the place Deanna Tamblyn would stand, watching over the old street. She wasn't there now. She was sitting in her mother's room with a tray of tea and two mannequins which were returning to life, and babysitting a mischievous, healthy two-year-old boy.

When she reached the top of Hanging Hill Lane, she pulled her shoulders back and lifted her face, feeling the wind on her skin, and tried to ignore her fear as best she could as she waited for her lift to arrive.

And so she stood, alone and okay, proud of herself for standing with her fear rather than running from it, at the top of Hanging Hill Lane.

She was alone, with nothing around her.

Nothing at all.

Nothing to her left or her right.

Nothing in front or behind.

And the nothing whispered.

'Whenever you need me, look to the stars, and know I am always with you.'

'Thank you,' Daphne breathed into the breeze as she felt an unstoppable bittersweet pain build inside her, pushing her fear to one side.

'You're going to be okay,' said the nothing in the wind.

'Perhaps,' Daphne smiled, and the grief felt a little different.

It felt as if the nothing smiled back before it blew away in the wind, dissolving into a million tiny pieces before flying down the hill through the leafy green trees into the woods below.

Daphne didn't feel brave, but she believed it. She had to; the thought of another inquisition from Mrs Hunter terrified her. And so she chose to believe she was brave out of fear, and the irony of it all made her giggle a little, and giggling made the fear give way further. It came back with the sound of an oncoming car.

The taxi pulled up and Daphne got in. In the back seat, Paulie waited with a beaming smile. They started on her new journey to a faraway land, where she would become stronger and be a force for good. But first, she would just enjoy being with Paulie. She looked at him and felt peace. 'You know what, Paulie-bird? I was worried you came into my story just to become a big nothing-burger. And you ended up being the most important thing.' She smiled.

Paulie smiled back awkwardly. 'Why have you started calling me that?'

Daphne just smiled and a colourful Paulie-bird fluttered through her imagination.

Every evening, she thought, she would look to the stars, and feel a connection with what she had lost. What remained would never be enough, but if her mother was with her somehow, if only in her past and in memories locked deep within her mind, it would be as close to enough as she could get.

The stars. A connection. It was the only plan she had. She would not dally.

As she sat in the taxi heading for the airport and Paulie drifted off on her shoulder, she pulled from her pocket the pages of her mother's book she had found in the woods. The final part of her mother's poem, the epilogue, as her mother had written in her book, had found its way to her, somehow.

Daphne straightened the creased pages, took a breath, kissed Paulie's sleeping forehead, and finally felt it was the time to read.

As she read her mother's epilogue, she couldn't help but feel a smile spread over her face. When she finished, she read it again. Then she pushed the paper back into her pocket, and the smile remained. It remained all the way to the airport.

Daphne and Paulie walked through Heathrow Terminal Three, Paulie's face swamped with awe.

'Look at the price of a coffee here. That's just nuts.' One of the wheels of Paulie's small case was stuck and he was struggling to control its direction as they walked. They stopped.

Daphne just stood, her smile still reaching both ears.

'You're really happy, aren't you? That makes me happy, too.'

The truth was she hadn't stopped smiling since she had read the ending of her mother's poem.

As they continued through the terminal, she heard a voice coming through the crowd. It was friendly, female.

'Excuse me. Daphne, right?'

Daphne turned. A brunette lady in her mid twenties sat on a chair holding a cup of coffee, her hand luggage by her feet. She was familiar, very much so, but Daphne couldn't quite pinpoint how she knew her. 'Hi,' she said.

'It's nice to see you smiling.' The woman smiled back and took a sip of her coffee. 'Off somewhere nice?'

'Yeah. A very hot, very sunny place.'

'Sounds lovely,' said the familiar woman.

There was a short silence, Daphne desperately searching her brain for where she knew her from.

'I'm Paulie.' Paulie extended his hand awkwardly. The lady shook it confidently.

'Nice to meet you, Paulie. I'm Joanne.' She looked at Daphne. 'I'm taking some time off, finally. Going somewhere very cold, on a bit of an adventure.'

The announcement came over the speakers. Daphne's departure gate was open.

'Have a lovely time,' Daphne said.

'You too.'

Daphne and Paulie walked towards their gate, Paulie tripping over his luggage as he started. A few steps later, it finally twigged in Daphne's mind who the lady was. She just hadn't recognised her out of her police uniform. She turned and gave a smile and a wave. Joanne Bach smiled warmly and waved back.

Paulie's face looked so stressed suddenly as they joined the queue, making Daphne feel nothing but more affection. Somehow, his imperfections just made him better. 'Nothing can go wrong now, Paulie-bird, we're here. We made it.'

'I know. It's just my first time. Why are you so smiley?'

Daphne's mind returned to her mother's epilogue. 'Just am.'

As they walked through the tunnel and the aeroplane entrance came into view, Daphne said through her smile, 'Fly, Corky, go!'

'What?' said Paulie as he shuffled towards the plane. 'You're weird.'

'I'll tell you one day.'

Settled in their seats, Daphne looked out of the window across the wing, the smile never leaving her face. The sun was low in the sky. As she spoke, mist appeared on the window in front of her mouth. 'Actually flying off into the sunset like a fucking cliché.' She'd booked the evening flight especially. She liked the private joke with herself. 'I'll be that if I want. My world, my rules.'

'Yeah,' said Paulie. 'Like a superhero. You'd be a good superhero. Where did you learn to be so friggin' magical?'

Daphne leaned back and smiled and her mind was flooded by the image of her mother, dancing to music under the accidental influence of the love salt, smiling a smile of pure magic. Daphne took Paulies hand and patted his palm affectionately. When her eyes met his, she simply smiled.

'What?' Paulie asked.

Daphne paused, and winked her eye, then stroked the hair on his head.

The engines roared and the sun was gold.

'I'll tell you later,' she said.

The Epilogue

Down at the bottom of the deepest ocean,
A million pieces; alone.
A bottle cork had arrived.
When an ocean of pressure
Squeezed them all back together –
The bottle cork had grown.
;
Up through the depths of the darkest sea,
Fly, Corky, go!
The bottle cork popped and flew.
Up through the surface.
Up to the sky –
And landed in its home.

THE END

The end of Hanging Hill Lane

Well, that's it for the Hanging Hill Lane trilogy. Thanks for making it this far!

I have no plans to return to Hanging Hill Lane now. I've made Daphne miserable enough.

There are so many more thanks to give. I don't know where to start.

Back to the beginning, I guess, the people who helped me with early versions of the early ideas, back when The House on Hanging Hill Lane was a screenplay that Covid shut down. So, thank you to my filmmaking buddy Tom Turner, and feedback buddy Tom Menary, for helping get all this started.

All my other feedback people, who take my ropey ideas and sentences and make them into something worthwhile. My development editor, Becker Jones at Jones Novel Editing. The editor who has been with me for all three books, who I couldn't do this without, Kathy Towns. My other editors, who have brought additional expertise and angles to the writing, Tracey Govender and Danielle Yeager. None of them read this page before publishing; these mistakes are all mine. My alpha readers, Isla and Paula. My beta readers, Alex Nisneru (read her books!), Leigh Kenny (read hers too!) and everyone else who has read an early version.

M.L. Rayner, for letting me take a comedy pot shot at his book in mine. Really though, everyone should read

Echoes of Home. It's a wonderful ghost story and Matt's writing is impeccable.

My crowd of author friends who I cannot list all of because there are so many, but here are a few... MJ Mars, Sarah Jules, Elizabeth J. Brown, Brianna Raine, Jim Ody, J.J. Maguire, David Watkins and of course Matt, Leigh and Alex mentioned above. Also, the wider community who are close to the authors and help us so much, including Trish Wilson, Sharron Joy, and Tiffany Koplin.

The Books of Horror group.

Mino, for the front and back cover paintings. Working with Mino is so much fun and that guy is excellent!

My wife, Vanessa, for the inside and chapter heading illustrations. Salamat!

Everyone who has read and reviewed these books, or passed them to a friend. I really appreciate it. Including you.

And everyone I've forgotten. I didn't mean to. Thanks!

About the Author

Philip Alexander Baker started his writing career as lyricist for indie band Lemanis, which released two albums, *Shell*, and *The Truth Behind the Push-Me-Pull-You*. Life as a filmmaker and screenwriter followed, including writing the award-winning *A Story for Happy*, and producing the British crime drama films *Killing Lionel* and *Card Dead*.

The Hanging Hill Lane series are his first books.

Twitter.com/Phil_Baker_
Facebook.com/PhilipAlexanderBaker
Instagram.com/Phil_Baker_

www.ingramcontent.com/pod-product-compliance
Lightning Source LLC
Chambersburg PA
CBHW051134190726
48290CB00006B/1836